GIRL CRUCIFIED

By R.C. Peris

WWW.RADIONMEDIA.COM

Girl Crucified

Text © 2017 by R.C. Peris

Cover and Interior Art by Radion Media, Inc.

Email: publisher@radionmedia.com.

www.radionmedia.com

Print ISBN- 978-1-946496-27-0: 1-946496-27-8

First Edition

Printed in the United States of America

Dedicated to the new chick life – S & Q. May you find your way in a hard world.

"A high degree of intellect tends to make a man unsocial."
— Arthur Schopenhauer, *The Wisdom of Life and Counsels and Maxims*

"Hungry man, reach for the book: it is a weapon."
— Bertolt Brecht

Chapter 1

The men were dressed in black and the women were dressed in white, and it symbolized their eternal separation. The Reverend said, "Man may enter the woman and man may claim ownership of her, but two souls can never merge into one body. Every man and woman is alone in the world and each weeps out of loneliness." The Reverend looked at the small sea of congregants cluttered under the red tent in the field. It reeked of manure and was pocked with gutted soil full of weeds and the occasional tall stalked sunflower that quivered in the breeze and strained to the light of the sky. They were waiting for more. They did not want to hear about the isolation of men and women. They came for something else – something no one has ever told them, but that intrigued them, making them wonder about the future of the world, the hidden history of the bible, and, more importantly, the flower between a woman's legs. "And God gave his only begotten daughter to save the world and not condemn it. We know about the son, the man who walked on water, healed the sick, and turned water into wine, and then died at the hands of the Romans with support from the Jews, and who hung on the cross and asked why he had forsaken his only begotten son. God told the son, in a secretive whisper as he hammered the nail into his wrist, 'I allowed you to die for political drama, but I will have a daughter, and when the daughter is born, she will die, like you, but for sexual drama. Man uses and women are to be used. That is the world. You die so wars can be fought in your honor. My daughter shall die so men can seek their pleasure. This is the way of the world. The daughter saves the world with her love and innocence and, though the petals of her flower are plucked and she withers back into the womb, she does not condemn the world. She does not dissolve into pessimism or anger. My daughter shoulders her burden and smiles to the grave.' " Many of the men in the straggling congregation nodded their heads, and some clapped, but most of the women were unsure of what they'd just heard. In seeing the reaction of the men, some became suspicious, but the Reverend smiled a smile as wide as the Mississippi, and her red hair fluttered like a flame in the wind, and she said, "I should know. I had a daughter."

Chapter 2

I stood on the hotel bed, legs on either side of the prostrate body that was feigning sleep, and considered my husband. I would have traced him with my toe if I thought I could keep my balance. His hands were behind his head and there was tension in his mouth. He was trying not to smile.

"If you smile, I'll beat you."

He managed to suppress outward joy, and I dropped down to my knees and straddled him over his stomach. He didn't have very much chest hair, and the hair that was there was the color of toasted chestnuts with a few grays swirled in. My favorite part was how the hairs narrowed into a thick line leading to his pubic hairs. I rolled to the side of him and let my fingertips trail from his clavicle down to the edge of the dark pubic region. My favorite part of all, of his whole body, was that small expanse of skin above the pubis, where the stomach narrowed. I called this area the butterfly because when I touched it with my fingers or tongue his muscles contracted and fluttered like white wings caught in the heat and thick light of noon. His lips parted slightly and his chest rose and fell just slightly quicker. I had made a study of the butterfly in the morning and it drove him mad and I was concerned we might get a phone call complaining about the noise. It was just my tongue on that small muscle area, and he acted like I was performing some kind of kinky sex act. It was now evening and I decided to focus on his penis, not that I have in any way ignored it in the week we have been married and the countless times before we were married, but because I haven't had a chance to gaze on it for long without him completely going nutty. He seemed to sense my gaze and opened his eyes.

"We don't have time," he said. "We have to be at dinner in an hour." He reached one of his hands down and twisted a segment of my hair in his hand.

"Get your hand off me and put it back where I told you to put it." He was really bad at following directions.

"Have you noticed that in movies they show vaginas but very rarely the penis?"

"Vaginas are better." His eyes were still closed, per my orders.

"I don't think so. I love your penis. I like the color of it, sort of like blushing oatmeal." I laughed. "Imagine the color of oatmeal and then the color of your flushed cheeks every time I spend too long gazing at you." My tongue slid down the thick shaft and then up and around the swelled mushroom like head. "You have a tiny vein running from underneath the head and down and around the back of your penis." My tongue circled around and back to the side. "Your balls are lopsided though." I laughed. "One is slightly bigger than the other. I like putting the smaller one in my mouth. It's like sucking on a lollipop. Should I put it in my mouth now?"

"No."

"What?" I pretended to sound hurt.

"Petra, would you come up here? I'd like to touch my wife now."

I didn't follow his direction immediately. I took my time and let my tongue slowly work its way up his body, neck and then his chin. He grabbed hold of my face in his hands. I let him kiss me but denied him my tongue and this made him hungrier and I laughed and lay back in the bed.

"Why do you do that?"

"Hmmm...."

"Deny me." His eyes, in multiple and complex shades of blue, were staring at me.

I touched his jaw and then rubbed my thumb on his lower lip. "If I don't, you'll consume me too quickly." He groaned and nuzzled my breast. He knew it was true. When we began living together, he lost all semblance of restraint in our lovemaking and was coming too soon and, even when we would begin again twenty minutes later, he would still become too excited and I would be deprived the pressure of his penis deep inside me. He always made sure I orgasmed, but it wasn't just coming that I enjoyed. It was the feeling of him deep inside me, and if I pushed into him hard enough, there was this feeling that we locked into place. I learned how to pace him and deprive him and give him just enough so that we both came and strained and moaned into each other at the same time.

"We should get dressed." He sighed. "I should have told everyone no."

We had been in California four days, and three of our nights have been spent with either a relative or a friend. Tonight, the fourth night, would be with his brother, who I was actually curious about because he was supposed to be some kind of financial wizard. I was convinced he was a white collar criminal. William begged me not to call him that to his face or suggest it, and I agreed, though I didn't promise, mostly because my filthy mouth and twisted mind did not easily restrain itself.

I got out of bed and untwisted the negligee that had gotten hiked up.

"You owe me three orgasms when we get back."

"Three?"

"With your tongue," I said.

"Well, that's totally possible. How many will you owe me?"

"Zero."

"That doesn't sound fair."

"Welcome to married life."

I turned on the shower in the bathroom and took off the negligee. William was watching me and sat up. "I love being married to you."

"Better than your first time?"

I was baiting him. He described his first marriage as "boring"; she was not faithful, and had had several miscarriages. He says it exactly like that, every time. It's the exactness that makes me suspicious and I intend, somehow, to figure out the truth of the matter.

He jumped up. "Let's get in the shower."

Bath time was my favorite. He was so good and attentive at scrubbing and rinsing my body, and he was quite good at shampooing. I was less good at washing him, as it usually ended with me giving him a hand job. Then we had to wash ourselves all over again.

I have a large scar radiating from my left shoulder down to my mid-rib cage from an unfortunate run in with a filthy prick. I'm not ashamed, and William, honestly, always kisses me there first. But I do not like questions or prying. As I already stated, William and I have a complex past.

The navy blue dress I chose completely covered the scar; however, when I saw William dressed I rolled my eyes.

"You can't wear that," I told him.

He looked down at his clothes in confusion. "Why?"

He was wearing a navy blue, high sheen, collared button down shirt.

"We match. We can't match. We're husband and wife, not mommy and baby."

William considered the statement, and then put his hands on my waist. "I wish you had been my mommy. I think that's going to add a new element to bath time with you."

I swatted his hands away.

"Stop. Forget I said anything."

William followed me out of the room and kept talking about how much he wanted mommy to spank him. I ignored him and looked at email on my phone as we went down the elevator to the lobby. He was still going on about mommy stuff when I went into the Japanese restaurant and gave our reservation information.

When we got seated at our table, I leaned over and said, "I had no idea you always wanted to fuck your mommy."

He looked alarmed. "No way. I just want to fuck you but, you know, pretending to be a mommy."

Sex was starting to make him demented. I think that was because he was a man. One morning I was eating a banana and he got so excited he wanted to feed me other fruits, like an orange, which was confusing because I had no idea what that was supposed to represent. I questioned him, and he said he just wanted to see me eat fruit. I was annoyed, as I really just wanted to eat breakfast in peace. I told him to go away, very far away, and so he went to work. He called me an hour later to ask me if I was eating fruit, and I hung up after pretending he had the wrong number. He called back apologizing for the wrong number, said I had a sexy voice and that his girlfriend was domineering and abusive and wanted to know if I could have phone sex with him. I told him to touch himself while I squeezed my nipples and got off on the sound of his voice. I put the phone down and kept shopping on Amazon as I made occasional moans. After I submitted my order for a new translation of Arthur Schopenhauer's philosophical works, I picked up the phone. He said the phone sex was great for him. I asked what he was in the middle of doing, expecting to hear, filling out boring forms, and he said executing a search warrant. I hung up the phone.

William's brother, Keane, was about four inches shorter, with thinning blondish hair, and was sporting a several thousand dollar gray toned suit with a red tie. Next to him was a young, much taller woman with an abundance of hot iron straight blue black hair, and fat, insect stung lips lacquered in glossy, iridescent lilac. Her name was Ty, though it was Keane who introduced her, as she was gazing at her cell phone without a single glance to us. William and I stood and there were handshakes all around. No hugs. William and his brother barely got close enough for a handshake. I was relieved there were no hugs, as I am not a person who likes human contact. I won't even get a massage as the idea of a stranger's hands on me gives me mild panic attacks.

Keane looked me up and down, narrowed his eyes, and then looked at William and asked him how married life was going. The skeptical appraisal was both curious and annoying and, unfortunately, I had to stew in those feelings as William and Keane journeyed to the past to revisit the magical land of Irvine, California, where they spent their apparently privileged suburban upbringing chasing girls, hanging out in malls, surfing on the weekends, and speeding down the 405. The waitress, clad in tight black everything, arrived, and Keane insisted on ordering for the entire table as he had just gotten back from a business trip to Japan and now considered himself an expert in sushi. After the waitress left, Keane went on to talk about mutual old friends from Irvine while I stared at my hands and tried not to appear bored or left out of the conversation.

Keane finally looked at me and said, "You got my brother to marry you. How did you manage that?"

The question was hostile and the sexual blur of the day was dissipating, which meant so was my good disposition. I didn't hear William step in, which was odd, so I decided all efforts at being bland and nice were done.

"William stalked me for many months, then begged me like a puppy dog to marry him, and, since there was no one better around, I said yes."

There was silence as Ty looked up from her cell phone, glanced at Keane, and then went back to gazing at Twitter. I didn't look at William, and I didn't really care, as he should have stepped in and verbally spanked his brother for asking such a question. Keane's eyes got both shiny and hardened. William started to speak, but Keane cut him off.

"Is that why you guys got married in Las Vegas?" Keane was still staring at me.

"No, we got married in Vegas because I wanted to get drunk and high." I gave a tight smile.

"She's making all this up." William sounded angry and concerned, though I don't think the concern was for me. And three quarters of my statement regarding our courtship and marriage was true.

"She's nothing like Madison, is she?"

"I don't appreciate you making a comment like that." There was a knife's edge to William's voice.

Keane smiled. "Sorry."

He then started talking about how he met Ty at the home of some multi-millionaire who lived a few blocks from our hotel in Laguna Beach. And that's how the rest of the dinner went: Keane talking about women, money, suit buying, and tie selecting, and dropping various Hollywood names as I stuffed sushi into my mouth and pretended like I didn't give a shit about anything. But there was also a familiar feeling resurfacing that made me feel both reckless and doomed. Thankfully, the evening didn't last too long, and I excused myself at the end of dinner and said I had a headache. I didn't even smile at Keane and barely looked at William.

I got to the hotel room and went straight for the mini bar. I hadn't drunk in three months but the thirst never really went away. It just got submerged like some kind of sand beast waiting for the worst time to resurface and consume me. I used to drink daily, and often before work, or if some kind of uncomfortable feeling nagged at me. I drank, like most people, because I was unhappy. This did not mean alcohol made me feel happy. I think Cary Grant might have called it a gorgeous thirst in some black & white movie from long ago. I'd have to agree with that description, as the first few drinks made me feel voluptuous, laser focused, and provided something to fill the void of the moment, the minute, the hour and possibly eternity. Alcohol is said to be a depressant, and in the first stage of the binge there is profound and overpowering hypomania that makes the world seem not only bearable, but remarkable, and your place in it fated. At some point, you end up in a pit and your desperation makes you reckless whether through breaking things, fucking things, or ending it all with a pretty bullet, a lazy leap off a convenient bridge, or just the characterless bottle of pills sitting in your bathroom cabinet that you mostly disregard until they become as beautiful and precious as an original Ming vase.

I downed four Grey Goose baby bottles and was so very thirsty for more. I saw five baby bottles of Tanqueray Gin and pulled them all out. I looked at the clock - 9PM. No sign of William. He was probably still with his brother trying to convince the less than handsome, vapid Keane that I was a real find, and that even though I may not present as well as the long ago, dead Madison who pleased the whole clan, he was far happier than he had ever been. I considered my week long marriage and assumed it would end at some point. I didn't put much stock in forever and ever or whatever other uncreative crap cropped up in pop songs. I suppressed an image of me decrepit and alone and very near rolling into a deep grave.

Before diving into the gin, I discarded my dress on the floor and found a tank top and jeans. I was more comfortable drinking clothed in case I needed to make my way to a bar or store to stock up. I always found it difficult trying to aim my feet into pant legs while sloshed. I opened the balcony doors and pretended to enjoy the soft, subtly salty, somewhat cool breeze wafting off and up from the Pacific Ocean surface, but I realized I didn't give a shit. Besides, the sea air only smelled good a thousand feet back and thirty feet up. Down on the shore and pressed into the asshole of the ocean you got strong whiffs of otter excrement, rotting barnacles, curdled trash thrown off some pier somewhere, and, probably even at night, that sickly coconut smell of sunscreen. I looked at the black expanse of the Pacific. I could only discern occasional frothy white foam.

"Hello, again." I wasn't trying to evoke Neil Diamond. I was just making an honest salutation to the old, slutty, cracked self that was suddenly in the room, looming in the shadowy corner, flashing her fangs and ready to destroy it all. I missed her. I really did. I spotted the lithium pills and anti-depressants on the dresser and flushed them down the toilet with only a hint of hesitation.

I twisted open the gin bottle and sipped. I had work to do. I booted up my computer and decided on a course of study that had been flopping in my mind for some time. I pulled up You Porn and perused. This was not for masturbatory purposes, though You Porn, along with Red Tube, were as remarkable an invention as the internet itself. I am sure that, if in the early days of DARPA, they had a sliver of premonition that a network of computer communication could lead to non-stop, unmitigated private pornographic viewing based on a specific sex act, the government might have kept the whole program private so lieutenants and generals in Alaska, Iowa or any embassy could jerk off at work without fear of being discovered by their wives. I wanted to study porn from an artistic and social perspective. I hadn't quite developed a research focus or hopeful thesis, but I didn't think that should stop me from venturing out and exploring.

The door opened and I didn't look up.

"What are you doing?" asked William with both surprise and frustration.

"Go fuck yourself," I said.

I had work to do. I clicked on the category of fisting and discovered other subcategories of vaginal, anal, double, lesbian, BDSM. I didn't know what to click first.

William was pacing. I kept drinking and clicking. I liked discovering the subcategories and thought there might be a research focus in that – the myriad of sexual activity all to achieve one five second orgasm, if you're lucky.

"Why did you just say that to me? Why are you drinking?"

"I wanted to. Answer to both questions."

"Is this because of my brother?"

He sat on the corner of the bed facing the round table where I was sitting. My laptop was turned away from him so he had no idea what I was looking at.

"You mean the asshole who insulted me? Nope." It had to do with the fangy, shadowy self in the corner who, I should add, was staring at me the whole time I was looking at porn. William sighed, and that's when I finally looked at him. I was learning things about him on this trip that I was not liking. He was far more wrapped up in what friends and family thought and did than he ever let on. In fact, he held the exact opposite position when he started sharing his life with me which, thinking back, wasn't much. He, however, knew too much about me, and not because I offered up my soul for his inspection but because he did a lot of fairly illegal following and researching. I was this blackish reservoir he had plumbed and navigated and he was this precious little puddle I sometimes dipped my toe into.

"I think we should talk about it."

After the events in December of last year and his insistent pushing of me into therapy he was more inclined to force discussion of things I preferred to ignore.

"I don't want to." Click. Click. Click.

He came over and grabbed the tiny gin bottle out of my hand and I slammed down the computer with the other. There was no need for him to learn about my research. He was very dramatic about prying my fingers off the green bottle. I wanted to laugh. It's not like it was a Costco size bottle. Once he freed one bottle, I stuffed the others into my pockets. He saw it and approached.

"If you even try to take the rest, I'm out of this room and going someplace else."

He sighed and, quite frankly, looked miserable.

"My brother was way out of line and I explained that to him, at length. You have to understand, my family were more in love with my ex-wife than I was."

Snap. I just caught him in a lie.

"You said you were never in love with her."

"I..well...it's true. Look I married her, she was a high school sweetheart. I obviously loved her at some point."

I sighed. I was sick of talking about a dead woman. Loved versus in love was a distinction unknown to me mostly because I had never loved anyone in my entire life so I had no real comparisons or experiences to draw upon.

"You don't have to explain anything. Go to bed."

He was quiet, and then busied himself around the room as I went back to clicking and sipping. I didn't seem to notice much of anything other than the porn, on mute, drifting before me like fantastic sparkling fireworks drawing me further and further into the fleshy, spectacular realm of bumping, humping, spitting, shooting, squirting, licking, and spreading. I might have had other words if the volume were on. Women were center stage. The men were secondary. There didn't seem to be any agonizingly long gazes at male genitalia, or faces, or chest hair, or...well, anything. Men were the creatures directing, stuffing, shoving, fingering, and performing a multitude of other activities that I couldn't remember, so I started taking notes in what was supposed to be my journal. Ill-used and useless, it had instead become my laboratory research notebook.

Around 3 AM I closed the computer and threw the many bottles of booze into the garbage and got into bed with my clothes on. I fell asleep and dreamed of widening vaginal holes that made room for fists and not much else. My old demented, slutty self in the dark corner did not sleep, I should mention, and she was making plans through the night to pull me back. She was like the puffed up Mafia. She wanted me. I'd like to think she missed me, but I knew she just wanted to feed off the crop of new feelings and emotions so she could chew, savor, and spit into a spitty, congealed mess of a cup she used for phlegm.

Chapter 3

There weren't many options for therapists in the White Mountains, so I called

the first one, Abby Baumgarten, and scheduled an appointment. She did children,

family, and individual counseling, though I think her primary focus was children as

her office was filled with toys, sandboxes, a doll house, and a puppet theater. I didn't

feel like a grown up in there. She was in her thirties with deep brown highlighted hair,

an unattractive fringy scarf tied around her neck, ballet flats on her feet, and a

strangely icy demeanor. I think she wanted me to be a child. I provided her my

background with edits and she had raised eyebrows throughout. Great. She asked for

a specific reason as to why I was in therapy, as if my past wasn't enough, and I told

her that I wanted to look for my long disappeared mother and to be "emotionally

prepared" for it. Those were actually William's words that I was borrowing, as I

figured they sounded therapeutic and might be easily understood by the icicle therapist

sitting across from me. She commended me for being brave. Shut up. I filled her in

about what I remembered of my mother. She demanded more. What did she look like,

she asked. Irish, I said. I shrugged. You know more, she said. Well, shit. Yes I do.

Although doing a full scale excavation on the first forty-five minute session with Elmo

staring at me from the shelf of crappy stuffed animals was not possible. I always

figured therapy was a slow, unraveling process. Apparently, in an age of impatient

health insurance companies, therapy had become drive-thru fast. She asked me about

William and I told her what I was willing to share. She asked me if I was afraid of the

relationship and I answered yes. She ended the session. It was so helpful. When we

reached the Arizona border, I felt sleepy and decided to sleep but William kept talking

about such disparate things as Syria, his stint in the Marines, Laguna Beach, Irvine, and his time at UCLA that I started getting agitated and went back to reading. Then he went silent.

"Don't you have any comment?"

"To what?"

William shook his head. "My life."

"Is that what you were talking about?"

William let out a soul-quivering sigh. "What happened to you in Laguna Beach?"

"Are you a fucking idiot? You were sitting right there while your brother did the jib jab right into my spleen and you said nothing."

"That's not true." He glanced at me twice.

"Okay. You said one thing." I wanted a drink.

"My brother acts like a jerk and suddenly you start drinking again, stay up all night on your computer, rebuff my effort to have sex with you twice, and have been ignoring me all the way across California to Arizona."

"Welcome to married life. And I've been meaning to ask you, why didn't we meet your parents?"

William said nothing. He seemed to be concentrating intently on a highway void of traffic. Oh, William, so obsessed with me for so long and you can't even claim me openly. I'm the grungy secret you masturbated to in your dark car as I blew men for money or gave free hand jobs by lakesides. I'm being unfair. You fell in love with me despite my past, my mental illness and my penchant for literature and philosophy. Or

maybe because of them. Alone, you are worshipful, but when confronted with your past
- that precious Orange County boyhood - you flinch. You can scrub me and scrub me,
but my history will never be clean.

"It's okay," I said. "Your parents are probably boring fuckers. Don't want to meet
them anyhow." I went back to reading and wished I could nap.

"Don't say that." His voice had a soft lilt of sadness. I suddenly wanted to fuck
him wildly as we drove down the vacant road, but I had to teach him a lesson. Bad, bad
William.

Our home in Springerville is nearly seven hours from the California-Arizona
border. Springerville is in the White Mountains in northeastern Arizona. It stretches for
mile upon mile upon rugged mile across a huge swath of land. There is snow in winter
and heat in summer and always the stretching shadows of the Ponderosa Pines. I'm
originally from Greer, not far from Springerville, but have lived in and visited many
places. I moved back to the White Mountains to discover my past, reluctantly and with
little enlightenment, and William left California to avoid his. We collided into each other
and things cracked.

William was taking the responsibility for driving and I decided to take the
responsibility for napping, at last. He kept quiet about California once we started the
hard trek through the Arizona desert. His denial and unrecognized shame was, literally,
out the back window. I woke up when we got to Mesa, where we stopped to stretch and
eat in thankful silence. Another long chunk of driving followed as the desert gave way to
dusty vegetation, canyons, rifts, and the Ponderosa Pines. We stopped again in Payson
at a Mexican restaurant where the tequila-thin Margaritas were that day's $1.99

special. I ordered four, not at the same time, but definitely in swift succession. William said nothing, and tried not to look at the drinks like they were rat poison and I was an approaching vermin about to lap up my own disintegration. I licked the ice cubes, chomped on them, and then traced my tongue along the inside of each glass. The waitress stood by the kitchen door, watching me with equal parts fascination and derision. Wait staff should never judge a customer. A customer's disorder should only be acknowledged to attend to it. Back in the car, I slept again, and did not awaken until Pinetop-Lakeside. Very close to home now. We whizzed through the reservation and kept going and then I could see the rounded tops of Sunrise Peak, Cyclone Peak and Apache Peak. We passed the turnoff for Sunrise Park, a ski resort owned and run by the White Mountain Apache. It was March, but snow was evident on the peaks. There was snow at ground level as well, though significantly thinned, blotchy, and at this point, more like lingering morning frost. William picked up speed and I wanted to remind him not to speed as they loved to ticket in this area, but it wouldn't have mattered since he was the Sheriff now. No employee is going to ticket their boss. As we approached the turn off for Greer, William slowed, as there were three cars up ahead that were stopped and I could see people standing on the street. Curious. There is nothing of any interest on the Greer turnoff. As our car pulled forward, I saw it, or rather, her, as there was no mistaking the breasts and pubic hair even from a distance. Set back from the edge of the road was a high cross hammered together with spiky nails and riveted with screws. You could tell the wood was knotty and rough. On the cross, like drapery, hung a woman with a trailing and mussed mass of nearly orange hair and almost matching pubic hair. Her wrists and feet were nailed to the cross. We were at a complete stop, and William was gazing in confusion and shock.

"Oh, look," I remarked. "A girl's been crucified."

Chapter 3

I told the kiddie therapist a good memory of mother Medusa. She and her friend from the bar they worked at in Pinetop were in our small Greer chalet drinking it up. I was sitting in the living room watching cartoons on very low volume, and mother and her friend were at the dining table about five feet away. Mother was talking about men she liked to fuck and said muscular confidence drove her mad and her friend, with fried split ends coarsely brushed around her shoulders, said it was dicks that drove her crazy but it had to be a big dick. Mother scoffed. Every woman likes a big dick unless they got a sensitive twat. What else do you like about a man? The friend thought and then shrugged her shoulders. Mother pressed. What gets you going? The friend said dicks. Mother said she liked men but hadn't found 'the man.' I turned around. Mother was still with my father who was out somewhere building a house for a construction company. How do you know when you've found him? Good question. It's just gonna hit you like a big thunk upside the head. They were quiet and likely thinking about the soap opera they watched before they talked. In it the woman goes deep in a kiss with a man and then declares with a heavy breath, You're the one. I didn't see her get thunked. Mother then asks, Have you been going to church? The friend said, Yep, and it's getting real interesting. What are you learning, asked mother. The friend takes a long drink of Bud Light. How to be happy. Where to find it. How to keep it when you find it. Mother looks doubtful. In church? In a church with God? The friend gulps again. That's what God is. Happiness. Mother asks, What do you do to find it? Oh, says the friend, we pray.

I stayed in the car while William got the miniscule crowd to back up and encouraged them to drive off. He had already called the station and was waiting. It was Friday and he wasn't supposed to be back at work until Monday.

"Vacation is over," I yelled out the window. William ignored me because he knew I was teasing him while secretly seething that our so-called honeymoon was done. With something as weird as a crucified girl on a state highway, he would be sinking into work. Maybe. Things move slowly in the White Mountains, and weirdness generally requires forensics and autopsies, neither of which could be handled at an advance level in these parts. Most testing got sent very far away, leaving the Sheriff's department to be the real detectives. And, being a real detective was slow going in a far flung area where people and places kept very basic hours.

Four patrol cars came along with an ambulance. Everyone stood around gazing at the poor girl except for William, who walked around staring at the ground. I couldn't tell if he was thinking or looking for something. I watched his baby blue shirt encased back and could see he was tense. Another two cars arrived with battery operated lights. It would be dark in an hour. William talked to every deputy and then pointed at me. A few heads looked over and two waved at me. I waved back, but had no clue who they were. A few minutes later, William got in the car and we drove off. Only the low hum of the car heater could be heard.

William was very bottled up when it came to work. I heard nothing about no one. When we became more intimately involved back in December, we were working on the same case, and even when it became obvious that my past was wrapped up in the case, he still wasn't particularly chatty. He went to his office and worked, and occasionally would give me a brief update. I'm in law enforcement so maybe that explains the hesitation, but I also think it was an issue of control and his interest in allowing me some level of sanity. William liked having a domain to which I was barred entry, but I don't think he realized that; he thought he was helping me and absolutely nothing more.

We got home and darkness was nearly sealed perfectly. There was only the light from a Gibbous moon and a few early evening stars. Our house, sitting empty, was barely visible until the headlights from the car lit up the wrap-around porch. William owned a fairly large log cabin buried at the end of a gravel driveway. I had a small chalet-style home in Greer, but was in the process of selling it. It sat empty, waiting for someone to buy it as a vacation home. Most of my belongings were now piled in his once orderly garage, and I do believe it gave him mild spikes of rage that there was a mess on his property. He was a neat, orderly person, and I was a maelstrom of chaos invading the eaves of his mountain palace.

He unloaded the car quickly as I turned on the lights and heat and lit the living room fireplace. I assumed he was hurrying so he could go back to work.

"Just leave everything. I'll put it away." I wouldn't put shit away.

And then my new husband of one week, who was the paragon of stormless demeanor, grabbed hold of my shirt, looking like he was going to spew harsh words until they got clogged in his tenderhearted throat. I furiously broke free of his grasp and then, for the first time since December, I slapped him hard across the face. But that didn't seem to be enough so I slapped him again. He looked so conflicted, poor thing. I took off in a huff and he followed.

"Go away, I hate you." I couldn't think of any other words for the emotions that were making me want to claw him and the walls.

"I love you." His favorite response.

"I don't care." I slammed the bedroom door shut but he opened it.

"What do you want?" he asked.

I thought about it. "I want you to fuck me," I said. William looked relieved and feverish. There was a lot of rolling around and straining on the bedroom floor until I got myself situated on top. Impaled. Long ago leaders would crash the battlefield and then impale their enemies. Tortured, exhausted bodies sliding down spears unto their death. I don't know why I thought about that as I moved with no beat or rhythm, just alternately languorous and frantic. I was trying to hit that spot except his hands and words were breaking my efforts. I leaned forward and covered his mouth with my hand.

"Keep your arms down," I breathed. Finally I could concentrate on the feel of him, the clean and opulent smell of his testosterone and beach-soaked skin, and the sound of strangled air through his nose. And then there it was. The familiar feeling of panic erupted. I pushed through it until knife sticks of pleasure went up from my pubis to my throat and I pressed harder into him. I was oblivious to everything except his crazy moaning. I fell off onto the rug and waited for my limbs to gain strength.

There is, after orgasmic sex, God in the infinite silence. He is nowhere else at any time. He is not at the point of death. Most people preparing for death don't open their arms to God. They cling to things in life. Even Jesus Christ did not embrace God. He spoke, from whatever energy he had left from a day of torture and condemnation, in a tiny voice to his father, "Why hast thou forsaken me?" It was a last ditch question to crack light onto his relatively short existence. It was, however, not a straining to God, and there was no silence, as there were cries of pain from others nailed to nearby crosses, whimpering women, agitated Romans and loud praying. You only get silence in life from pleasure, and the greatest pleasure is from a deep, thudding orgasm. And God appears. For a few brief moments you are beautiful, special, loved, amazing. A true offspring of God. You want to be in that moment and nothing else. You want to dissolve into the universe and be no more. This only lasts a few seconds, as the brutal world comes rushing in as little God hearts go rushing out.

My liquid limbs hardened and I was back to being an awful, spiteful bitch.

"Are you leaving?" I asked, trying to sound impatient.

He was still huffing. His God pleasure tended to last longer than mine. "Do you want me to?"

Not really. I wanted to lick his chest and arms and neck and face. He would have let me, too. And then he would have sucked my clit until I was one with God. But I had to be fierce. I couldn't let him get away with that wife comparison shit his family and friends did. He had to be punished.

"Whatever."

"I hate when you say that word. As much as you read and think, you can't come up with a better word?"

"For indifference? 'Whatever'is a splendid word for indifference. I thought you would have to work. Weird shit."

He was staring at the ceiling. His affable face was a little darkened by confusion.

"Who would do something like that?"

"A religious nut. She couldn't have been up there long. Her body looked fresh."

"It couldn't have happened more than an hour or so before we saw her. There didn't seem to be any drag marks on the soil. That cross was handled by multiple people in a quick timeframe."

"Multiple footprints?"

"No. All raked over."

"But the major observation I made," I said, "was that it was at the entrance to Greer. How odd that three major crimes in less than four months occurred in a tiny city with one bar and no gas stations, and with virtually no crimes of interest for decades."

William clapped a hand over his forehead. "I hope that you are in no way involved in this."

Loud guffaw. "No way. How could I be?" I set the matter aside. Nonsense. However, I was starting to wonder about Greer. Soon it might become an interesting crime hotspot for tourists. I wondered if it would increase my property value or hurt it.

"No, I'm not going anywhere," he said, and searched for my hand across the carpet. I let him find me and in finding me I got ravenous.

"You must fuck me again."

"I must?" His voice sounded amused. He pulled me by my hair towards his mouth. I clamped my mouth shut. This frustrated him and he became more eager and ardent. I laughed. I had power in denial.

Later in the night, as his nude body lay under fluffy blankets and he snored ever so slightly, I got out of bed and went to my laptop to do my research. I noted that anal was quite popular and crossed categories and sub-categories. Women just got drilled. The actresses did a good job feigning immense pleasure; however, I was sure most were high on cocaine. There wasn't even a hint at initial, modest pain. They were pleasure automatons.

I remembered a guy I had a conversation with at a Starbucks in Phoenix. I had connected with him on a dating website. His profile had stated he was forty years old, but there was no doubt he was well into his fifties. In a low voice so as not to be overhead by jerks in headphones battling away at their laptops, he shared that he once got seduced by two lovely female friends who lured him to their apartment and wielded a dildoe. He was hesitant at first, but he finally allowed them their passion and they induced crescendos of orgasms.

"With just a dildoe?" I asked.

"One blew me at the same time." His face was dreamy and off in some dildoeland where women made men come by stuffing their asses. I didn't believe him. Not at all. I heard plenty of other stories of men being wooed by women in similar fashion. Some of the stories might have been true, but I checked Red Tube and Your Porn for any videos where women were bonkers about anal rape of a male and, sadly, none could be found. I figured that those videos were probably on more specialty websites. A fetish within a fetish. Mainstream, however, was women getting pounded in the ass and often with multiple dicks. A woman was a thing to be used in every hole, repeatedly. And endlessly filmed, even in intimate acts like masturbation.

I still didn't know what I was investigating or why I was viewing porn like an addict. It was linked to a decision to stop taking medications and start drinking. Mentally unstable alcoholics have been known to develop sex addictions, though I couldn't accept this was an addiction as I wasn't gaining any pleasure from it. It had more to do with determining who manipulated female sexuality. I did run across a category of porn considered romantic, claiming to be created by women for women. It was boring stuff because it seemed passionless. There was a lot of licking and languid moving, and some barely registered orgasms, and then it was over. Riveting. I preferred the pushing around ass-slapping to that crap. I closed my computer and yawned.

I was not tired enough to sleep (I knew it was related to not taking my meds), so I took a nosedive onto the couch and scanned the pile of books on the table before the fireplace. I grabbed *Ulysses*, flipped a few pages, crinkled my nose and set it aside. *The Iliad* was there. I wasn't in the mood for Greeks. I picked up Schopenhauer, who was carted along on vacation. I turned pages, stopped, then turned some more, and then it was there like a worm in Eden's apple: the purpose of our existence is not to be happy.

You could be a monk. That could get you out of the problem. Maybe. Being a monk is about dialing down desire and will. That wouldn't make me happy. Not at all. Still, I could live with not being happy. When I was suicidal in the past, it was about confusion and obliteration of self. Mostly confusion. It wasn't the struggle of Sisyphus* up the hill. (*I'd rethink this analogy. I don't see it as being truly applicable here.) I'm fine not being happy. I've just grown annoyed with mysteries and I have an unfortunate tendency of disassembling in their midst.

I went into the bedroom at 4AM where William was turned on his side. I touched his cheek but he did not move. His breath was silent. I knew that soon I would hurt him by taking a chunk out of his soul. This made me sad because he was the only person I had ever loved.

Chapter 4

The red hair was always held fast by a ponytail or a twisty, messy bun. She liked wearing tight, sequined shirts but would pair them with grungy jeans with holes. Mother didn't spend too much time in the mirror, and I never saw make-up on her, but occasionally, her lips would be glossy but it rubbed off quickly onto her Pall Malls and beer cans. She wasn't ugly. Mother was just blanched like white rice before it's cooked. Irish. Mother would say, I'm Irish, that's why I resemble scone dough. Rice, I insisted in my head. Dough is yummy. There were freckles too. A connect-the-dots picture on her face. One time she was napping on the couch and I took my finger, lightly, and followed the freckles. I could make any picture on her face. A pigeon, a truck, a telescope, a bear. She'd wrinkle her nose and my finger would disappear, fearful of awakening the beast. Then she'd snore and it was safe again. I wanted to make a book but the freckles wouldn't connect. I wanted there to be a book so I could read her. Who are you, mommy? Tell me who I am. Then her eyes flashed red. Get the fuck out of my face. Go to your fucking room. You little bitch. Get the hell out of here. I ran to my bedroom and slammed the door. Back to Matilda. Back to Alice bouncing down the rabbit hole. It wasn't enough. Busting the door open like a devouring mouth. Her hand grabbed my hair, spun me like a sack, then landed across my cheek and I was down. Wished I had a rabbit hole to spin into. What the fuck were you doing, she screamed. Trying to read you, I cried. Shut the fuck up.

I awakened at 6AM. Two rough hours of sleep. William flopped, sighed, and got out of bed. I think he was smiling at me. I was concentrating on the increasingly interesting ceiling. He showered and dressed and then left the bedroom. He was so disciplined. Always pulling it together to go to work. One day after the next. When I had been a child abuse investigator, I frequently called in sick to work or tried to find excuses not to go into the office. Obviously, it wasn't my destiny to work with the Department of Child Safety, though I had no idea what I should be doing. William claimed not to like working for the Sheriff's Department when I met him, and had refused a promotion to Sheriff, but then became Sheriff after a leave of absence. Maybe law enforcement was his destiny. Was mine to serve the public servant? Should I wake up every morning, make him breakfast, pour coffee into a shiny thermos, give him a peck on the cheek, do laundry, vacuum, make lunch and drive it to him at the station, and then shop, clean some more, prepare dinner, talk about his day, then go to bed? Shit. I yawned thinking about the boring litany of tasks. Maybe I am taking the word "wife" too literally.

There's another kind of wife. Solid Sarah. The Bible speaks of her beauty, though it is her duty and loyalty to Abraham that glows from the thin pages. They were rootless. Drifters on a swift stream of life granted by God. Into Egypt. Abraham whispered, "Tell Pharaoh I am your brother." Good Sarah nodded and did as told, and Pharaoh took in lovely Sarah and began to torment her. And Sarah suffered and cried. Pharaoh carried on like a blasted schoolboy until Sarah said, "Abraham is my husband. I am his beloved wife." The Pharaoh laughed. "I care not," he said. And he continued to torment her and then an angel struck him. Smack. He became ill, and then he realized that she was the wife of a Chosen Man. Pharaoh gave her his daughter Hagar as a slave. That's what you did in that crusty piece of sand land. You gave slaves. But the story doesn't end there. Abraham bangs Hagar and she gets pregnant. Sarah remained a good wife. Supportive. You are selected by God, Abraham. I shall always love you no matter who you fuck. And then God graced Sarah with the birth of Isaac at an age when her ovaries should have been tiny, pocked, shrunken fruit bits emptied of life. Sarah was another kind of wife. I hadn't determined what kind of wife I was or wanted to be. I should just fall into him. Protect my husband. I should go around to stores and talk about my husband. Enjoy saying the word. Husband. My husband this. My husband that. I couldn't do it. Not because I didn't love him. I couldn't do it because I couldn't carve out a segment of myself, polish it up, and then hand it off to him and the world. Here you go. Have this. No. I am me and no one gets to twist off a piece of me like a hunk of bread.

"What are you doing?" I demanded. He was leaning on a counter in the kitchen staring at a cup with coffee.

"Drinking coffee."

"No, shit. Why are you going to work? It's Saturday and it's still our honeymoon."

He looked perplexed. "You're kidding right? You saw that freak display. I can't ignore it and bury myself in you until Monday."

I opened the refrigerator. It was nearly empty except for butter, wilted celery, and mustard. I needed gin. I closed my eyes and imagined drinking the velvet liquid. It would burn my throat, but then there would be that glowing heat in me. I needed a deep drink.

William had his eyes fixed on me. An unfilled face and morning fresh. I kneeled before him on the granite tile floor and unzipped his pants.

"Petra, you don't..."

"Shut up," I said. I took him into my mouth and it didn't take long for me to drink the balmy, viscous fluid from his penis. I didn't normally swallow. That morning I did. I was a different kind of wife.

But then I wanted him to leave because semen could not take the place of liquor. William left, reluctantly, and I flopped on the couch with thoughts of pretty tumblers all lined up, overflowing with liquor. When I heard his car drive off, I got showered and dressed and then wandered the house. Everything was as clean as if a maid had come right before we left for California. I wouldn't clean it even if it was dirty anyway. Laundry needed to be done, but I hated that. Starting the load was fine. It was transferring the clothes to the dryer and then folding that sucked. I went to the den and watched *Game of Thrones* on Amazon. I re-watched part of Season 2, and then figured I should stop when I felt the need to masturbate to Littlefinger and imagine a tiny, aquamarine dragon balanced on my shoulder.

I called William.

"Is something wrong?" he asked.

"Why does something have to be wrong if I call you?"

He was quiet. "It doesn't, and I enjoy hearing from my wife." He said "wife" with some delight. "But you aren't that type of woman. You never just call because you want to hear my voice."

"That's sad." I considered what else to say because why I called would not make him happy. "Any interesting cases?" I laughed slightly and hoped he thought I was being playful.

"No."

"What?"

"I'm not sharing the case with you."

I collapsed back on the couch and considered my options for the rest of the day. With no job, I had nothing to do, and even if the house was dirty, William did not like me cleaning it as he felt things were never cleaned properly if I did it. He didn't even like me washing laundry. I didn't understand the concept of separating the colors from the whites. I needed something. A little crumb of something.

"Do you know who she is?"

Silence.

"No, we don't."

Mystery woman. "Real redhead," I said.

Silence.

"What?" He sounded curious.

"Her pubic hair was red."

No comment. He was waiting. I could hear faint noises of the station in the background. I heard phones ringing. The receptionist, Gladys, talking into the phone. Then Marge, loud and clear.

"You and Petra are coming over tonight, right? Serving up prime rib and wine. You didn't forget did you?"

Marge was a senior deputy who was overly nice and desperately wanted to be in your business. If I saw her in the supermarket, she seemed to make mental notes of what I was buying. Once I saw her in the Target in Pinetop, and she gazed too long at my basket swelling with bras, socks, bargain books, pretzels and gummy bears. I was not drinking then and was constantly chewing on candy in an attempt to satiate my divine thirst. She had also dedicated two years to finding William a wife. I was never short listed or invited to her gatherings. Fuck you, Marge.

"I did forget and yes, of course, we will be there."

"Fantastic." Marge seemed energized.

I groaned. "I don't want to go."

William said something to Marge and then directed his attention back on me. "We're going," he said.

"You can go without me."

William was losing his patience. "I don't have time for this. Be ready when I get home. It's been nice talking to you."

"Wait…"

He was such a jerk sometimes. I figured I had one more question before he hung up.

"Don't you think it's interesting that the spikes went through her wrists and not her hands?"

Most stories of stigmata and depictions of the crucifixion feature the spikes going through the hands. St. Francis of Assisi had wounds on his wrists. The Romans crucified people with spikes going through the wrists. The hands weren't sturdy enough to hold the weight of a person.

There was silence again. He was considering his response. "And what do you think that means?"

"Somebody did their research or…"

"Or?"

"Or God has a daughter who just died for our sins. I'm going to the store. Bye."

I put on a light coat and got into my SUV. I called the new editor at the *White Mountain Times* on my Bluetooth. Her name was Charlene Boxborough, and when you spoke to her, she squinted and seemed to be seriously analyzing what you were saying. She usually offered you candy at the end of your statement with little comment on what you actually said. I'd been writing for the *White Mountain Times* for about two years. I was also a photographer. There was a shortage of news in this area, to say the least. Most of the articles that appeared focused on teachers or law enforcement officials who were retiring, deaths in the community, local festivals, snow and ski news, and school performances. Blah and blah. When there finally was an interesting story, I was the center of it, and a victim, so I never had a chance to write about it. Another wannabe journalist picked up the story and interviewed me. Since January, I got a few emails each month asking me to cover stories, but I had little interest. Once again, there was an interesting story.

"Hulllooo?" Charlene liked to elongate words as if you couldn't understand her unless she did.

"It's Petra. I wanted to pitch a story." Right to the point.

"Yeesss..."

"Did you hear about the girl crucified in Greer?

Charlene took a deep inhale of breath and then sneezed. "I heard about it but didn't believe it. It's true?"

"Saw it with my own eyes."

"Dear, dear...I can't see how you can do the article. What will Sheriff Armor think? You would have to interview him. I can't see him sharing with you."

"Why not? I'm his wife. We talk." I was getting a smidge defensive.

"Course you do, it's just...go ahead. Work on the article. If Sheriff Armor decides he doesn't want to muddy up your marriage, I can get someone else to. Did you get a picture?"

Muddy up my marriage? "What?"

"Picture of the girl."

"No, Charlene. We were driving by and then it became a crime scene. I don't think my husband would have liked me snapping photos of a victim. Too much muddy mud."

"Hmmm...very strange crime, is it not? Some people are complete bonkers mad. If I say screw loose, that implies they can be fixed with the proper instrument and force. Not true."

"Everybody is crazy."

"You think that, do you? I don't. Many people are well adjusted, even tempered, loving people. No trace of crazy. Like your husband, Sheriff Armor."

Not me. She didn't mean me.

"He's not that sane."

I shouldn't have said that. But he wasn't completely sane. He obsessed over me for two years. Stalking me. He was nice about it. He was nice about his obsession. I'm not sure that means he's sane.

"Really?" Charlene's voice contracted a tinge of excitement. Tell me more. Tell me more.

"I have some errands to run. I'll get the article to you by the weekly deadline."

I clicked off without a response. No trace of crazy. Like your husband. I was married to him a week and it was already getting annoying.

I turned onto the Greer exit and drove slowly down Main Street. There were tourists walking on the side of the road, looking around as if they were on Main Street in Disneyland. I pulled into the parking lot of Molly Butler's. I hadn't been there since December. It was early afternoon and there were only a few people in the bar. The restaurant had opened for lunch. I could smell rich sizzling meat. There was a new bartender. He was about 5'8" with a goatee. He had greasy looking, longish hair pulled back with a blue rubber band. His teeth were pointy, like they had been chiseled. He had a cordial manner. Good for a bartender to have.

He leaned on the counter and looked at me evenly.

"What can I get you?"

"Gin and tonic."

I looked around. I didn't recognize anybody at the tables. Likely tourists. At the end of the bar counter, I saw Kevin "Loose" Marbles who used to own a construction company in the Phoenix area and then retired to Greer. He was called "Loose" because he had a habit of picking up female tourists and locals and carting them down the hall to a hotel room. Molly's also had lodging. Loose rented a room each time he drank there. He said he was afraid of driving under the influence, but most of us knew it was done for the convenience of pick-ups. Loose, for a man in his mid-60s, was attractive, had lots of battleship gray hair, a smile that oddly shot little darts of warmth up my vagina, and was a good conversationalist. He waved at me and walked over with a drink in his hand.

"Haven't seen you in a while. Did you give up the lovely liquid?"

The bartender set the drink in front of me and I took a long, very long drink and sighed.

"For a moment."

"Heard you got married." He sat down next to me.

"Word gets around."

"Word has it you married the sheriff."

"The word is astute."

"Word has it no one at the station likes you."

I snapped my head towards him. "Where did you hear that?"

"It's just the word. The word is everywhere." He was looking out the window. There was a squirrel in the leafy, overly branched tree.

"It's a lie. One person there likes me."

"Who?" He looked surprised.

"The Sheriff." I finished off the drink and waved to the bartender.

"Good point. He's a good catch for you. Sane, too."

I rolled my eyes. "Shit. He isn't Andy Griffith and this isn't Mayberry."

"Sure, it is. This is small town America and he's Mr. Perfect."

"I'm done with this conversation."

"Okay." Loose went back to staring at the squirrel that now held a leaf.

"Did you hear about the girl who got murdered?"

Loose pursed his lips and exhaled as if he was trying to whistle.

"I saw the photo of her face on a website. I knew that girl."

"How? What website?"

"I once took her to my hotel room. It was like having a feral cat in there. I had to pay for damages when I checked out. Boy, never had a woman as passionate as that. Just never happened."

"When was this?" I was trying not to sound excited.

"I'd say back in January. Not long after the New Year."

"What website?"

"Hmmm...?"

"What website?"

He shrugged his shoulders. "Just a blog. Someone was driving by and saw her. Took all these photos. Might be viral now on social media. Who knows?"

"Did you get a name before you fucked her?"

"Hey, no fucking. Just wild love."

"And when you expressed this wild love, did you get her name?"

Loose was staring at his empty glass, and then looked up and squinted at a drink special written on a glossy blackboard. Greer Fog:$3.95.

"Hey, Tim, what's a Greer Fog?" The bartender came over and pointed at my drink. I nodded. He took Loose's empty glass.

"We're trying to get rid of old stock. It's just a mix of about six liquors. Fogs the brain." Tim started preparing my drink.

"Funny." Loose didn't look amused. "I'll stick with my usual."

Loose patted his paunch that was more pronounced now than it had been in December. Without clothes he probably looked elderly. I didn't think his status as 'loose' was going to last much longer. We didn't say anything as we waited for our drinks and gazed out the window. The squirrel was gone, and sunlight was smearing the tree with a yellow, glittering light. Tim put the drinks in front of us.

"Did you get her name?" I pressed.

"Ah...Lotte...and then another 'L' word...Lenyom..."

"Lenya."

Loose peered at me over his drink glass. "You knew her? It was Lotte Lenya. Feral cat."

"You said that." I drank some more gin fire. "I didn't know her and I'm guessing the name is fake."

"Why do you say that?"

"Lotte Lenya was an Austrian singer and actress who was married to Kurt Weill. You've heard the song "Mack the Knife?" Probably Bobby Darin's version. Louis Armstrong did the English version first. He added Lotte Lenya's name to the song."

"Interesting." He wasn't interested.

"I'm curious why she would choose that name."

"Maybe it was just her name."

"Statistically it's possible but not probable."

"Sure."

Loose kept peering at me. Too much booze for you, Loose. Then I remembered something.

"Lenya was Brecht's favorite singer."

"Who's Brecht?"

"They don't teach shit in American schools. Never mind."

"What are you saying?" He closed his eyes.

"There's a Brecht out there directing the play. Lotte on the cross. All staged."

"Who would do that? Who would do that in little Greer?"

"Maybe someone from Greer with a big mouth and a big plan."

"Shit. The last person I knew from Greer with a big mouth and big plans was you. Did you kill poor Lotte?"

"I did not." I finished my drink and stood.

"Do you have an alibi?"

"The Sheriff. We were driving back from our honeymoon"

"How did that go?"

"Shitty."

"What's his dick like?"

"Better than yours."

"How?"

"It's not small and shriveled."

I motioned to the bartender to tally up. Drinks were reasonably priced at Molly's. My bill was less than $20. I paid with cash in case William saw my credit card bill. He didn't need to know I was starting to drink at Molly's again.

"Nice talking to you, Loose."

"Likewise. Let me know if I can defy your judgment on my penis. I'd be happy to show it to you."

"I'll think about it."

I left Molly's and headed to Pinetop to shop. There is no high end shopping there. Only Target and Walmart. There is also a collection of antique shops and boutiques popular with the tourists. I needed to waste time and think. Without the lithium, careless spending habits were waking up. Without the sale of my house and no money coming in, I was relying on my savings to pay my credit card bills. I should have been prudent and spent nothing, but I was never prudent. At least, not when I wasn't medicated. I stopped at Old Time Antiques and looked around, figuring out what to buy. There were clusters of junk, lines of jars with old buttons and screws, old toys that were rubbed and worn from a child's hyperactive fingers, pocket watches, dolls with missing eyes, tables and chairs with gunk, and stacked pictures depicting vomit-inducing, maudlin scenes. I sorted through them and then found it: a large photo of Bertolt Brecht framed in pewter, and emblazoned with "Hollywood," etched hills and an ocean. It was $45 and I happily bought it. The cashier asked who it was and I explained.

I'm not into dramatic criticism. I only know what I read and can understand. Brecht was German, and though he claimed to be working class, he was raised middle class in a fairly spacious and well-furnished house. When World War I broke out, he was still a school boy and said, "You're an idiot if you die for your country." I first read Brecht while in the Army and stationed in Afghanistan. It was idiotic to think dying was a good idea, no matter the reason. You couldn't convince most soldiers otherwise. They believed their lives had meaning as long as they were going to die for something called "a country." But back to Brecht.

He started medical studies, though was quickly enraptured by the theatre. He wasn't simple. No cheap psychology for him, and he wasn't about propaganda. He connected with Kurt Weill who wrote music for his plays. The Brecht/Weill partnership is more well-known than one might think. *Cabaret*, the Broadway musical by Kander and Ebb, is heavily influenced by their contributions. . Brecht's work was focused on the social milieu, but I think it was also deeply personal. When I read *Mother Courage and Her Children*, I wasn't struck by the anti-war protestations. I was struck by the main character's self-awareness. She knew she was fucked. Life was fucked. Her place in the midst of everything was fucked. Her children's future was fucked. She knew it all. She accepted it. Being fucked.

I drove to Fry's Market and considered fucking. Lotte Lenya getting fucked by Loose. Getting fucked on the cross. And all the fucking I was watching for my porn project / non-project. And how fucked I've been throughout my life and how my fucked-upness began with mother. The red-haired bitch who didn't want me. The Medusa who drove father away. The slut who fucked men so loudly I thought she was getting

murdered, causing me to flee to the closet. I looked in the rearview mirror. I'm fucked.
You wouldn't know it by looking at me. Pretty, pulled together, the appearance of
functioning, a ring on my finger. Don't be fooled. I'm fucked. At least I'm aware of it.
Awareness of reality seems less pathetic and pitying.

I bought food. Actual food to eat. Not that I intended to cook anything. William
would do that with his competence and efficiency in a kitchen setting. In any setting,
actually. It was hard to think of where he would be out of place. Maybe a surgical
theater, though he would be an intent observer and might learn a skill he could utilize
under different circumstances, like an injury on a camping trip. His competence is
what I liked least about him, probably because it seemed inauthentic. Having known
him for two years, I still didn't know who he really was, and each time I got it into my
mind to figure it out, he got that benevolent glow and I sunk into petulance. Let him be
competent, I told myself. At least I was being fed. I bought several bottles of vodka and
gin and thought of where I could hide them in the house. On the journey home, I
distracted myself by listening to 70s pop music and thought nothing of fucking, being
fucked or girls nailed to crosses. One needs multiple breaks throughout the day from
thinking, I guess.

It took three trips to unload the car. I removed the Brecht photo last. I decided
not to hide the alcohol, and placed all the bottles on the nearly vacant alcove bar.
William might not notice something hiding in plain sight, or so I hoped. I poured a
drink and sat on the couch with *The Threepenny Opera*. Brecht was, somehow, more
profound with vodka. I lost time because I heard the door open, and William was
standing in the entryway, hanging his jacket and carrying a thick file. At first he looked,

distracted, but when he saw me, he smiled widely. I didn't say anything and went back to reading. He sat down on the puffy leather chair next to the couch and placed the file on the table. I stared at it, wondering if he would leave it alone long enough for me to sort through it.

"Hi, honey. Welcome home," I said in a *tremolo* tone. He eyed me closely as if he were evaluating me for a beauty contest.

"Don't do that."

"What? Look at you?" He was smiling again. Oh, one day William I will get to the bottom of that good humor.

"Evaluate me." I was getting pissy.

"I wasn't. I was just noting that you seemed preoccupied and I was wondering what caused it. What did you do today?"

I threw Brecht at him. He caught it and flipped through the pages. "German theatre, all day?"

"Don't be so crass as to think he only impacted German theatre."

"Why does German literature always put you in a funk?"

"Why are you never in a funk?"

He threw Brecht back at me. "I am in a funk, frequently. I just do a better job of keeping my emotions in check than you."

"Why? Why do that? Suppress your emotions?"

"That's what you need to do in life. You can't just say whatever enters your head or do whatever you feel like doing."

I felt like he was lecturing me. Probably for the Keane fiasco.

"Why do you do that with me? Why can't you freely express yourself with me?"

William leaned forward and rubbed his eyes. "I don't know."

I was expecting him to say he did express himself. Surprising honesty.

"We need to leave soon." He got up and headed towards his office with folder in hand.

"Don't leave. I was talking to you." I walked behind him. He turned on the light to his office and sat at his desk. He stared at the file. I wondered what was in there.

"How about later, Petra? I don't think this will be a two minute conversation."

"How many minutes?" I leaned down on the desk to look him straight in the eye. I saw the usual kindness, but I also saw annoyance. "What do you want to say to me, right now? What do you want to do? Murder me?" I pushed his shoulder. "Say it."

"Petra."

"Say it." I pushed him again. Harder. He grabbed my hand and squeezed it.

"Why are you drinking? Where are your medications?"

I pulled my hand from his. I could take it. Self-awareness.

"I got upset."

"About?" He tried to reach for my hand again so I moved away.

"Your family and friends. I get shit here too."

"From who?"

"It doesn't matter."

"First of all, it was only my brother who made an inappropriate comment about you, and I addressed that with him at dinner, and after dinner at length. I didn't introduce you to mommy and daddy because they're mean people and loved my ex-wife far more than I did. It had nothing to do with you." William stood up and laughed. "So this whole moody shithole you've been in, along with the drinking and the decision to stop taking your meds, is because you're feeling sorry for yourself? You're an idiot. Sometimes. About ninety percent of the time you are the smartest person I know and then the rest of the time you're an idiot."

I didn't like being called an idiot so I walked away. He didn't chase after me as I went to the bar and poured another drink. He came out of the office and tried to pull the drink from my hand, but I cried out and fought him. He gave up.

"What would make you feel less sorry for yourself?"

"A different past."

"You're stuck with the one you have. Why can't you focus on the present and future? Life is easier for you when you take your medications."

"What's our future?"

William sat down on the couch looking slightly like a puppy dog teased with a bone. "What do you want it to be?"

"I've no career, and there really aren't options for me around here. There's nothing to do. There's no theatre, no universities, no art galleries with non-mountainous forest pictures. There's fuck is all there is. I have two options. I can drink or buy groceries. I could also be your sex slave. You'd probably be fine with that, but I got bored in February from being holed up here and fucking you. It has nothing to do with you. I just need more. I...I..."

I started crying like a young girl who was just cast aside by her equally young boyfriend and realized that life was not only unfair, but that pain is a part of it. William did not rush towards me or say anything and that made me cry more. I was quite sure he was regretting the whole marriage proposition. It seemed good, in theory, for someone who had been sexually obsessed with me. The reality was that I was a pain in the ass, and having me around all the time was likely crushing his soul. My crying began to subside and I poured another drink.

"What would you like to do?"

"I don't know," I said.

"That's part of the problem. Look, I understand you should probably be in New York or London going to the theatre, having artist-friends, and doing whatever it is intellectuals do. Right now, however, we're here and you need to figure out how to make this time in our lives meaningful to you. Self-destruction is not the answer. We need to leave for Marge's." He stood up and tucked in the part of his shirt that came loose from sitting.

"That's it? You're not going to tell me what to do?"

William looked disappointed. "I would never tell you what to do. Why would I do that? The answers to your life lie within you."

"William…"

"Hmmm…"

"If your wife were alive, would you swap us and would you fuck her right now?"

"No. To both." He still wasn't smiling.

"Would you fuck me right now?" I walked towards him.

"We have to leave and sex is not going to get you out of uncomfortable questions of your existence."

"What about if I wanted to fuck you because I loved your cock?"

William looked away.

"What about if I wanted to fuck you as an existential answer? What if your cock was the answer to the world?"

William said nothing. Still not looking at me, he pulled me into his arms and then did nothing other than allow himself to breathe in the scent of my hair, his face buried in the messy, chestnut blur. Through his embrace, he was trying to make clear to me that sex was not a solution to any life dilemma. That was something I was still trying to learn. After a minute or more he kissed me, and then said we had to leave.

On the drive to Marge's he said nothing but kept his hand over mine. I was struck by the fact that before I began living with him, we talked a lot more and I threw insults like rice at a wedding. It was all foreplay, certainly, and many days I miss the banter, but we now communicate in other ways that are more personal than words. We communicate in nonverbal ways that confound me because they affect me more deeply both physically and emotionally. What we say is less important because words are inadequate to express the multitudinous feelings I experience in his presence. I have no words for most of the feelings, and love is just a shadow word. Most people use it too much, and carelessly. People might say, "I love pasta," or "I love football," or "I love my wife," even though you are cheating on her. The word "love" conveys little, and I'm not affected by the word when William says it to me. What I am affected by are his eyes that deepen and lighten in color like a diver of the deep sea soaring up from the abyss onto the surface, or his proximity and the delicate palpitations he induces, or how he takes my hand into his like it is made of porcelain, or when he is angry how his fingers tighten on my wrist but never enough to hurt me. Sometimes I think I want to curl up at his feet like a sick cat and other times I wanted to slap him and watch his skin turn red and then fade to the color of a cow's pink tongue. Sometimes I feel like I can't breathe, like I am running into exhaustion. And other times, like on that drive to Marge's house, I feel satiated, and that swirling messy self inside me is unimportant.

Marge lived in a wooden planked house that appeared small from the outside but was more spacious inside, and she had a dining room table that sat twelve. Marge liked to entertain, but she also had four children, and when they brought over friends, a large congregating table was required. I used to call Marge "Frumpkin" because she was stocky and boring. She did a few nice things for me, prompted by William, so I stopped the name calling. When we arrived, she ecstatically hugged William, her boss, a little too long, then grinned tightly at me and led us to the dining room. Her greeting of me was less than lukewarm, and I made a mental note to start calling her Frumpkin again.

Marge's home was like any family's in Smalltown, USA, where the income was solid but the status never reaches middle class. Adorning every open space were photos of her children, with an occasional one of her husband and herself. I noted cruise photos where Dan, Marge's husband, was wearing Bermuda shorts, a Hawaiian shirt and flip flops, and he had his arm around a beaming Marge. They sported identical loopy smiles. Dan was bulky, though calling him fat would be misleading, as the bulkiness existed in his arms, chest and legs. He gave the impression of a former wrestling devotee who consumed too much protein for his newly acquired sedentary life. Dan was an elementary school teacher, and when he shook my hand, he also gripped my forearm with his other hand.

"Awesome to meet you," he bellowed. "Marge has told me about you." He had an out of proportion cheerfulness that likely went over well with his students. I vaguely wondered what Marge had told him.

Marge was bubbling over with excitement, as if William had never been in her home or she hadn't seen him for years.

"Have a seat," Dan said as he pulled a chair from the table. "Do you drink wine? I have red or white."

I smiled at him like he was an attentive dog with a wagging tail.

"I'll take both."

Dan was still smiling. "Really?" The smile hardened slightly.

I sat and listened to Marge talk to William. She was talking about women he met, and women she had tried to set him up with. One woman got married and one broke up with her boyfriend. There was other news, but my ears felt stuffed with silly details. William frequently peered at me above Marge's head, with his mouth tilted warmly and mischievously, but would then glance down at Marge to ensure her he was paying attention. Dan set two wine glasses before me, one holding a purplish garnet liquid and the other a crisp camel-colored one, and I took turns tasting them as I continued to watch William. He was still standing, and Marge led him around the family room pointing out more pictures of the children. The dining area was generous and graced with a fireplace, and above the fireplace hung a huge framed poster of a house emanating butter-colored light and surrounded by spring. It was a Thomas Kinkade print and I hated it. Art should be more than a pretty picture.

"Sweetheart, dinner is nearly ready."

Dan was wielding a large spoon and calling for Marge. The smell of the meat was, appealing, and there was a smoky undertone that mixed with the root odor of potatoes. Dan emerged from the kitchen hefting a roasting pan with a hunk of roasted meat. He set it down and came back with a bowl of mashed potatoes, a small dish of horseradish cream, and a platter of overdone green beans sprinkled with the crispy onions you usually found capping a green bean holiday casserole. Plates were laid down and my wine was topped off. William and Marge took their seats while Dan continued to fuss. William placed his hand on my leg and Marge pretended not to notice. I wondered how long we had to stay.

Dan started carving the prime rib, and it was a lovely pink inside. The dinner went on predictably. I was a piece of fuzz getting sucked up into the vacuum of domesticity. Marge and Dan went on about their children who were with grandparents in Show Low for the weekend, the brilliance of the older child getting an A in Abnormal Psychology, updates on neighbors and mutual acquaintances with William, and their upcoming cruise to Baja. Marge even mentioned that Dan was getting a teaching award for being so dedicated to his students. William then commended Marge for being such a good deputy. It was all so lovely, except I wanted to vomit and might have stuck my finger down my throat if my stomach wasn't already quivering with meat and sticky potatoes. And then it got worse.

"William, when are you going to have children?"

I did not look up from my limp garlicky green beans, though I felt eyes on me.

"We're considering it," chimed William in a pleasant voice.

I looked at him in disbelief, but fortunately, he was still staring at Marge and Dan was looking at them. We had never discussed it, and I had never expressed an interest in having a child. I did not want one. Not then, not ever. I didn't understand the burning need to procreate. I didn't like children and found them boring and tedious. I had no religious convictions to push me into procreation, or political views that defined my existence by my uterus. Not only did I not want the burden of parenthood, but I also cringed at the thought of childbirth. It was a disgusting process and I hated that women became this mass of straining flesh with a living thing inside them. Besides, you never knew what you were giving birth to. *Rosemary's Baby* had a tremendous impact on my views of pregnancy.

William deftly changed the topic by discussing the latest news at the station. There was, however, no talk of the crucified girl.

The dinner went on for another half hour, and then William said I hadn't been feeling well earlier in the day and so he needed to get me home. There were hugs all around, and this time I was engulfed by Marge and Dan. William pulled out of the driveway and I connected the Bluetooth and played The Police at a high volume. William turned it down. I turned it up. It went on like that for a few minutes until William got frustrated and turned the car screen off. I folded my arms and stared at the cones of illumination formed on the road by the headlights.

"Do you have anything you want to tell me, William?"

"Don't panic or freak out about the child comment. I needed to tell her something."

"Why not the truth?"

"That we haven't discussed it? Who gets married and doesn't discuss children at some point, usually before the marriage?"

"We do." I wanted the music back on.

"Good point." William became quiet and concentrated on the bleak road. "Do you want to hear my opinion on the matter?"

I didn't say anything because I was afraid of what I might hear.

"We can do whatever you choose."

I felt some relief, and then a surge of tenderness for him.

"Thank you."

We continued our journey home, and then I remembered that I had forgotten to share the important news I received from Loose.

"I was in Greer today and ran into an old acquaintance. He said he had sex with your victim, the girl on the cross. He remembered the name she provided."

"What is it?"

There was growing excitement in William's voice, leading me to conclude that they hadn't identified the victim.

"Lotte Lenya."

William didn't say anything, and I realized he probably had never heard of her.

"Do you remember the Mack the Knife song? She gets mentioned in there as one of Mackie's murder victims. She's a real person though." I explained the history of her that I knew, including that she was Brecht's personal diva and Weill's muse. William was quiet, though I could tell he was in serious thought.

"She was one of Mack the Knife's murder victims...can you tell me exactly who Mack the Knife is without you becoming overly literary?"

"A serial murderer. A cold-blooded gangster. How's that for unliterary? I could discuss the murder ballad tradition in 17th century Germany. Incidentally, the Mack the Knife song was dirge-like in *The Threepenny Opera*. When the play came to the US, Louis Armstrong converted it to jazz, and that eventually led to Bobby Darin's version, which is upbeat and, well, fun."

"Why would someone take the name of a murder victim?"

"Hang on. Lotte Lenya lived to a ripe age and outlived both Brecht and Weill. She died in New York. She wasn't actually a murder victim. Armstrong was friends with her and added her name as a tribute. A macabre tribute, but a tribute all the same."

"Our victim took the name of a once successful singer? That's less interesting. I wonder why that name."

"I don't know. You're the detective."

"Petra..."

"Yes?"

"I don't want you snooping into this case. Please, stop."

I stared at the lights on the dashboard. "Why?"

"I want you to be safe and sane."

"Gotcha." The reasoning didn't make any sense, as I wasn't safe or sane with or without murder cases.

We got home shortly after nine. William said he was tired and was going to bed early. I told him I would stay up and read. He kissed me fully on the mouth, with tongue but devoid of passion, and then closed the bedroom door. I went into the den where there was a large screen TV. My laptop was on the table and I opened it. When I pulled up the internet, You Porn was the first open page. I started clicking videos and then realized how boring it was to view porn without allowing arousal to be triggered. For the first time since November, I allowed myself to masturbate to one of the videos. I was careful to keep as quiet as possible so as not to disturb William. He would be angry if he knew, and that realization made me feel guilty and shameful and triggered my need to watch more degrading porn. For nearly two hours, I was caught in a terrible loop until I forced myself to slam the computer shut. I had also turned the volume on twenty minutes into watching when I realized porn was no fun with sound. I hoped William had remained asleep. I went into the bedroom, put on pajamas and got into bed. William stirred.

"Hey, what time is it?"

"I don't know, late. Go back to sleep."

I squeezed my eyes and hoped he didn't touch me, but that is exactly what he did. He pulled me alongside him, and then in his sweet, undemanding way, started making love to me. However, his tactic abruptly changed, and he began pressing vigorously into my clitoris, causing me to flinch. It was already sensitive and overused. I didn't want to push him away, but all sexual feelings had been drained from me. I allowed him to go on and started faking pleasure. It was the least I could do. I had dark thoughts that he might have heard the porn and was now punishing me. It might have been paranoia. I kept on faking.

Lotte Lenya #1

As most of us do, I grew into sex. Mother reminded me that she was granting me my freedom to explore.

I was homeschooled by a tutor of unique focus. He was an intellectual of the past who was versed in Latin and Ancient Greek, could recite Shakespeare, quote the Bible in Koine Greek and Hebrew, and speak seriously of Dickens and Melville. His knowledge of math was only marginal, which meant that the bulk of my education was in literature and languages. When I was seventeen and his services were coming to a close, I seduced him. He was not surprised, as we had developed a strong appreciation of each other's minds. I led him to my bedroom with no fear of being caught. Mother was out of town and there was only the housekeeper, Graciela, somewhere in the house napping, as it was siesta time.

Mother would have approved of my decision. She could be startlingly open-minded at times. His name was Macheath, though I wasn't aware that it was a false name until I was fourteen and we began our trek through German literature.

"You are Mack the Knife? Why such a brutal name?" I placed my hand over his.

"He may have been violent, but he was also dapper, genteel, and squeamish. We are all violently deep in the dark soil of our soul. It's not our capacity for violence that's interesting. It's our ability to disguise it, frame it, or utilize it that makes us interesting."

Macheath had a gentle demeanor. He also had a ferocious intellect. He was in his forties when I was seventeen, and his dark hair had thinned ever so slightly over the years. Outside my bedroom, I kissed him, and though I prodded with my tongue, his mouth did not open. I was confused.

"Don't rush," he said.

In my bedroom and on my bed, my sexuality unfolded languorously and Macheath took no more than I was willing to give. He was undemanding. He only wanted what I wanted, and when I was ready I pulled him close to me, breathed in the vague mint and cinnamon smell of his skin, and felt a brief sharp pain that gave way to warmth as I expanded, opened, and tightened. My limbs grew gluey from the viscous fluid that clung to Macheath. I became conscious of his breathing and the alternate pained and tender looks on his face. I placed my forehead on his chest and he wrapped his arms tightly around me and convulsed. I felt strangely proud. He left and returned with a towel and cleaned me. There was blood, though not too much. Macheath looked slightly queasy, and I laughed as I remembered that Mack the Knife was squirmy went it came to blood.

"Am I Jenny Diver?" I asked, confidently naked on the bed.

"I think Lotte Lenya. A remarkable, creative woman and muse to a remarkable, creative man."

"Why are men always turning women into muses?"

"Women are so beautiful."

"Men can be. Western civilization hasn't properly valued the male body since the ancient Greeks. Men can be just as inspiring to female art as women are to male art. I know why men don't like being muses."

"Why don't we?"

"Men don't like being gazed upon. But they constantly gaze upon women. We're always on display. It's almost predatory."

"You are on display now, before me. Do you feel threatened?" He stroked my long hair.

"Not at all. I feel treasured."

"I do treasure you and your fine mind. A most voracious mind. Your ancient Greek is subpar, however."

I laughed. "If only I had a better teacher."

I pulled him close to me and we again began our gentle journey. This time, I was more confident and more aware of all the twitches, pulses, and electric zings in my body, and Macheath was less composed and slow limbed. The accelerated pace had me running uphill, and because I felt so confident with him, I plunged over the precipice with no fear. What a remarkable thing an orgasm is.

"Fancy gloves oh, wears old Macheath, babe, so there's never, never a trace of red."

Mother came back two days later and interrupted our garden of sex. She stood in the doorway of the study and observed us without speaking. I kept my nose in a book on Nazism, and Macheath continued to read an essay I had written on *Moby Dick*. When she left, I nudged him with my foot. He didn't move towards me but smiled.

For the next few months, we would merge together whenever mother was gone. Often, I resented her presence because she caused distance between Macheath and me. I think mother knew this, as I caught her glaring at me a few times.

"You're graduating," she said with finality.

"Yes." I stirred a cup of hot chocolate.

"Macheath's services will be ending. Be sure to write him a letter of thanks for all the years he spent teaching you." She walked away and slammed her sitting room door.

I went back to the study as tears slid down my freckled cheeks.

"What's wrong?"

"What will happen to us when I graduate?"

Macheath fiddled with a button on his cuff. "I've taken a position in New York City. I leave in two months."

I set the cup down. "Take me with you."

Macheath looked sad, and then shook his head. "I can't, and your mother already has plans for you."

"What are you talking about?"

"I'm not sure. She did tell me she was bringing you into the business. I don't even think she intends for you to go to college."

"What's the business? What does my mother do?"

Macheath considered the questions. "I don't think I know. I've heard things, however, and I would rather not discuss it with you."

I placed my hands on my hips. "You have to tell me."

"She might be involved in...sex trafficking."

I staggered and then sat down swiftly. I hit my back on the chair and my lower back muscles seized. "What are you saying?"

"You've never wondered about your mother?"

"Only as a child does. I never suspected anything illegal or unsavory. I couldn't possibly become a part of that."

"You may have no choice." Macheath capped his pen.

"You have to take me with you to New York." I touched his arm and he pulled away. There was the look of fear set in his face. "You have to," I pleaded.

"Let's discuss it when your mother is not in the house."

Four days later mother left again, and Macheath and I sought sanctuary in my bed. My cheek lay on his bare chest as he devised a plan to help me escape. "I live in the French Quarter. I've sold off most of my belongings in preparation for New York. Your mother will be gone the day before your last day of instruction. When the housekeeper is sleeping, we could leave in my car with your bags, pick up the rest of my things and then head straight for the airport. We can leave my car in the parking lot. Your mother doesn't know about my new position so she won't know we've headed to New York. It should work." I kissed and kissed him. Mack the Knife was saving me.

When he fell asleep I went into the hall and saw the housekeeper sweeping. Over and over. The same spot. Odd. I went to the kitchen, got two bottles of water and went back to my bedroom. Macheath stayed until evening weaved its way through the swamps, and then he left to avoid the housekeeper seeing his car in the driveway.

When mother returned, she said very little to me and retreated to her sitting room. It was unsettling to think of her involved in sex trafficking. There wasn't a single clue I could latch onto that would explain such a dark and strange existence. She was very religious, and claimed to spend hours in her sitting room praying. Her frequent trips might have aroused suspicion, but she claimed she retreated for religious reasons. The only thing that could not be explained was money. We were well-off, and lived in a fairly spacious home surrounded by equally well-off neighbors. Mother was able to afford Macheath for years. We had a fulltime housekeeper. I had no idea where the money came from. None.

On the day of my escape, I packed a suitcase and stuffed it in the closet so the housekeeper would not see it. I was nervous but excited. I wondered in what state Macheath was in. I went into the study and waited for him to show up for the final lesson. I sat until 9:30 AM, and then began to feel a strong sense of danger. Mother walked into the study.

"We're going for a drive," mother said. She was dressed in slacks and a blouse. Conservative and elegant.

"I'm waiting for Macheath. This is the last day of instruction."

"He'll be late. We're going for a drive."

Macheath was never late, and my breathing started to become rapid. I could see my chest rising up and down like some kind of quivering mongrel about to get beaten.

"Where are we going?" I asked as I strained to make my voice sound calm.

"Let's go." She turned and the conversation was over.

I followed and got into the Lincoln. My body began to crumple and I became small in the passenger seat. We drove further into the swamp until the roads went from asphalt to dirt. After nearly an hour, mother pulled up outside a small shack that partly hovered over the swampy morass. There was a small dock that extended from the shack, and there was a pale blue rowboat tethered to it. I noticed there was a humongous SUV also parked outside the shack. I had so many questions, but I had lost my voice. Mother said nothing. She waved me into the shack. I walked in with a great deal of fear and apprehension. The shack was dark, and curling shadows lived there. There were two men, muscular and grim, standing in the middle of the shack. I could see that one of the men was holding a gun. The other man was wiping his hands with a soiled towel.

"Let her see."

Mother waved her hand and dismissed the men. They parted, and I could see a bed with a metal frame, and on the bed laid a bloody, naked male body. I walked very slowly forward, and I could feel a horror broiling in the pit of my bowels. When I was at the foot of the bed, I screamed and tried to bolt, but one of the men grabbed hold of my body. I couldn't flail my arms, so I kicked with all the strength I had. It wasn't enough to free myself of the man's grip. His arms were firmer than steel. Eventually my legs went slack and I began sobbing. On the bed was Macheath, and he seemed to have bled to death from the disgusting wound between his legs. His penis and testicles were completely gone.

"You can't just run from me. You're my daughter and you'll do what I want."

Mother had nothing more to say, and the man holding me let go and I fell onto the dirty floor. I was contorted and wretched. Mother said nothing more, and as I was picked up and flung back into the Lincoln, I thought of part of the lyrics from Mack the Knife.

Now on the sidewalk lies a body just oozin' life, eek, and someone's sneakin' 'round the corner, could that someone be Mack the Knife?

It became very clear to my young mind that we all die, that one day my body would ooze life like Macheath's, that I had loved him, but the love caused his demise. I was doomed. We're all doomed. The love between a man and woman is profane, imperfect, and only distracts us from the unfortunate reality of life. We are alone, and no amount of love could bridge the gap between our soul and another's soul. Sex destroys. So began my life of destruction.

Chapter 5

Mother began to change. Not a huge tidal change. She stopped wearing torn jeans. Gone went the cheap sequined shirts. She cursed less. She drank less. Mother began to modulate her voice, and she could express more than hostility when she spoke to people. Soap operas were no longer the usual TV diet. Sitcoms were played. Dramas unfolded. Horror screamed out of the TV speakers at night. Comedies were allowed. She still didn't laugh. She was changing, except her attitude towards me remained the same. I was a scab. An annoyance. A leftover of my absent father. I required care and she didn't want to care for me. She mocked my constant reading. Sometimes she kicked me out of the house, locked the door. I wandered to the edge of the forest. Too afraid to sink into it. I might get lost in its inky maze. Might have been a Minotaur in there. A dual bodied ruffian itching to have me lead him out, into the hard light, so he could swallow me. I stuck to kicking cluttered pine needles, inhaled the scent of sticky pinecones, sat on the porch waiting to be allowed back in. Wait, wait, wait. Then mother opened the door with no words. I was back to books and cartoons. In between, I eyed her and noted the changes. A Bible secured a spot on the coffee table. Curious.

I sat up, angry. Dreams were disturbing my sleep and I felt a heaving in my chest. I knew it was because I stopped the lithium.

Moods were circling like sharks. It was morning, I think. Quite early. William was next to me. He sniffed, shook his head wildly for two seconds, and then solidified back into a restful pose. I loved looking at him when he slept. I loved the freedom to gaze on him without him withdrawing. How unfair that he thought he had a right to memorize me while I was blocked from openly looking at him. If I fought with him he would relent and allow the gaze, though he kept his eyes squeezed shut. Strange creatures, men. My fingertips hovered right at his hairline. Just a few more gray hairs on the sides, barely noticeable unless you were counting. His hair had lightened a trifle. When I first met him, his hair was the color of chocolate mink, but it began fading and it had become pale chestnut. It was probably due to the threaded gray. There were a few lines on his face that had become pronounced, mostly along the corners of his eyes. His skin crinkled when he smiled and I liked it. I did not want a husband with a boy's unlined face. I touched his jaw and stroked the sprouted whiskers with my fingertips. I used to describe his face as bland. That was when I thought he had no interest in me. Then I desired him, and the blandness eroded as a vexatious, handsome face emerged. Things are beautiful when you love them. Things warp something sunk in you when you love them. I rested my cheek on his chest. I was so awful to him. Sometimes I think I was bad to test him. To trace the boundaries of his love. Or to get what I felt I deserved – no love.

His hand swirled into my hair.

"Good morning." His voice was still thick with sleepiness.

"I was gazing on you." I wanted him to know.

"Again? I still look like I did a week ago."

"It's my right. As your wife." I was adamant about that.

"Fine. You may exercise your right." There was a lightness in his voice and I looked up and saw him smiling.

"I need you to do something for me." I had been thinking about it for weeks.

"Anything," he said playfully as he squeezed my nipple.

"Not sex related. I'm serious. Can you do some kind of search for my mother and father? Any details about them should be in the original police report concerning me."

William had opened his eyes and was staring fixedly at the ceiling. "I could. I'm not sure I want you going down that rabbit hole."

"I have to know."

"I'm just trying to protect you."

"I know." William had always been very protective, which, at times was charming, though it was also aggravating because I was not some egg in a carton that could be easily crushed with the wrong movement.

"I'm not sure how much I can find out. I will try."

"Thank you." I kissed his cheek except that wasn't enough for him. He drew me to his mouth. With no bipolar meds, hypersexuality was taking up residence in my body. Obviously. I didn't think William was actually initiating sex. However, the gesture gave me a zingy pleasure and I straddled him. He didn't mind. Not at all. It was one symptom of bipolar that caused him little concern. Had he known about my deep forays into porn he might have thought twice. As we moved into each other, I had a weird thought about Heloise and Abelard. Heloise, who lived in the 12th century, was brilliant and needed an equally brilliant teacher. Abelard, a philosopher and theologian, was able to that fill position. They fell in love and began a sexual affair that was scandalous for that age. Heloise became pregnant. They fled Paris, were secretly wed, but Heloise's uncle actually wanted her to himself and had Abelard brutally attacked. In fact, Abelard was castrated. When I learned of that I became enraged at the uncle who only did that to punish Heloise and less Abelard. How do you punish a woman who had found sexual fulfillment? Make sure she never has it again. Abelard became a monk and Heloise entered a convent. For twenty years they exchanged impassioned letters, and when they saw each other again they knew that they still loved each other. Their love was the meaning of their existence. They were one, even without physical connection.

As I felt William's breath on my neck, I wondered about physical love and how important it is or should be. Sex may be the most ineffective way of connecting. There may be other, more lasting bonds. And yet, like Heloise, I found a complete untangling of my past sexual frustrations and torment with William. It would be cruel to be denied of it. My recent sexual obsession with porn had triggered my own self-imposed denial. I made a note to make the password on my laptop extremely hard to crack. Committing to excluding porn from my masturbatory endeavors seemed too great a request, just as giving up alcohol for life was too extreme to ponder.

For the next two days, I occupied myself with reading, thinking about my mother, and recalling the plethora of traumatic events from my past. I wasn't pitying myself or chiseling out despair. I was excavating, digging into a grave of the self. When I could think no more, I read Schopenhauer. I obsessed over Schopenhauer as I lied on the couch in the den, waiting for William to come home and give me news on the two people who created me.

Schopenhauer was sued by a woman who claimed the philosopher pushed her as she stood outside his door. At the time, Schopenhauer lived in an apartment building in

Berlin. He spent his days reading and writing. Like most vigorous thinkers, he required quiet. A large blanket of noise blotting quiet. And then came Caroline Marquet to wreck it.

"Oh, hello, Arthur," she would say in a mocking tone as she passed him in the hall. "What are you doing today? Philosophy?" Caroline had a wicked laugh, and Arthur knew she was making fun of him. She was the kind of person he liked least in the world – an idiot. Caroline considered herself an optimist.

"Arthur, look." She extended her hand which held a drinking glass. "My glass is half full. Wait, let me take a long drink of the cool water." She gulped and then stared at the glass. "Why Arthur, I think my glass is still half full. Isn't that amazing? I could empty this glass now and it would still be half full." Caroline's laugh was loud and tinkling, like little brass cow bells.

"Go away, you infernal woman."

Arthur wanted her to die. He imagined her being taken out by some maniac with an ax. How delightful it would be to see her hacked to pieces.

"What's the matter, Arthur? Are you getting frustrated by the nothingness in your glass? Or is it sexual frustration? That must be it. You've no wife or girlfriend. I heard you got a servant girl knocked up, and the little baby died not long after being born. Must have driven you mad. How are you satisfying yourself now? Do you jack off to memories of your servant, or do you think of other women, like me? I know you jack off all the time. I can hear you. You have pathetic orgasms, by the way."

Arthur stepped away from her and slammed the door. He attempted to read Kant, but he was distracted by his hard cock which was mysteriously erect after the taunting by Caroline.   He moved his hand up and down quickly as he tried to focus on the bosom of a woman he saw on the street a few days prior. He imagined burying his face in her tits, but then an image of his mother interrupted him. He quashed it in repulsion, and then thought about the servant girl and how lovely it was having her legs wrapped tightly around his midriff. He tried to hold to that memory though he still couldn't ejaculate. That's when Caroline began to unfold in his mind, except his goal was to punish,not pleasure her. He imagined pulling her head back and then spraying semen all over her face. It worked. He came all over the silk chaise and his pants. He tried wiping away the milky dots and streaks with his fingers but it became a smeary mess. He got a towel and attempted to be more methodical in his cleaning. It didn't work. There were distinct stains. Arthur could live without a pristine chaise. Perfection was a stupid thing to expect in life. The problem is that his mother sat on the chaise when she visited, and Arthur did not like the idea of her sitting on his semen stains. Whatever. He went back to reading Kant, with whom he thoroughly disagreed.

The next day he went to the market for bread and fruit and brought the goods home to make breakfast. Arthur was not overly indulgent when it came to food, as his passions were elsewhere, primarily in philosophy and sex. He ate his Spartan breakfast and began writing about man's will and how the will caused the destruction of happiness.

Around noon, he decided to take a break and lied on the chaise to nap. Soon, however, he found he was hard, so he figured he could quickly masturbate and then rest.

Arthur focused his mind on a woman from the market. She had just bought potatoes and walked towards the street when she stopped, set the basket down, and then lifted her long skirt to scratch her ankle. Arthur could see the vibrant outline of her calf that tapered into her narrow ankle. If Arthur had been a poet, he might have written something. Instead, he was a philosopher, and since philosophy wasn't about specifics he tried to explore happiness and the many ways we make ourselves unhappy. As Arthur thought of the woman's calf and the tormenting possibility of sticking his penis deep inside her, he became happily loud and vocal. He forgot he had neighbors. Just as he was about to erupt yet again all over that imperfect chaise, he heard a pounding at the door. The banging was insistent and urgent. Arthur groaned from the pain of stifling an orgasm, put his penis back within the confines of his pants, and opened the door to a blisteringly mad Caroline. Arthur was so annoyed at seeing her face that he wanted to punch her. To keep himself in check, he thought about exploding all over her plump face.

"You disgusting pig. I was trying to nap, but all I could hear were your piggy moans. You're filthy, do you know that?"

Arthur felt like he wanted to murder her. In order to keep himself from doing anything too dramatic, he pushed her. Caroline went backwards two steps as her eyes broiled with anger. Another neighbor came out of his apartment.

"Caroline, Caroline, is anything wrong?" The neighbor was a stocky man with a large bloom of wiry, black hair.

Caroline looked at the neighbor and then looked at Arthur who was still drowning in hatred for her. She developed a splendid idea in two seconds. She began crying and then fell onto the floor like a balled up rag.

"He pushed me. He pushed me. I'm so frightened."

The neighbor rushed forward and kneeled by her side to sooth her. Arthur was annoyed and alarmed. There was no reason for Caroline to fall on the floor. He had barely pushed her. He just wanted her gone, away from his door and out of his face with her abusive taunts. Arthur slammed his door shut and hoped Caroline would finally leave him alone. This was not the case. Caroline filed a lawsuit against Arthur. The complaint read – Tortious Interference with a Woman of Delicate Means and Demeanor. Caroline claimed to be afraid of Arthur and fearful for her very life. Arthur paced and cursed in his apartment after he read the complaint. The more he thought of ugly Caroline, the more he wanted to weep. He eventually collapsed on his chaise where his tears mixed with old semen stains. Then he stopped. This was part of life. Bad luck, anger, the annoying will of others slamming up against your own, sexual frustration, the deepest yearning for what felt like erotic desire but might be something far more inexplicable, a need for love but knowing that what you get will never be enough. Fuck it all. Life was confounding. He didn't give a damn about glasses being half empty or half full. For a man near death with crazy thirst, half a glass of water was not enough. It just wouldn't quench the unquenchable thirst. And for a man nearly retching from oversaturation of water, a man who chugged a brimming jug, he didn't give a damn about that glass. Empty or full, it didn't matter. It had what he did not need. Pessimism flowered from a pile of contextual shit. If Arthur's needs had been met, he might never have written about philosophy at all. But in his straining, yearning, desirous, angry mood, he had to accept that he was fucked and find a way to not be miserable. He would become a happy pessimist.

After reading the complaint, Arthur wrote for nearly eight hours on pessimism. When he was done, he felt better. The writing felt personal. He did not think that there were millions of fucked people out there who needed a way to deal with reality and not feel like slashing their wrists on a daily basis. They, too, wanted to be happy with all their willful desires. Arthur also accepted that the more unintelligent a man is, the less mysterious existence seems to him. Optimism was for dimwits.

William came home with no news of my parents and a refusal to discuss the crucified girl. I served a pasta dinner and I was commended on my culinary efforts. I informed him that I had also done the laundry and unloaded the dishwasher. He smiled and patted my hand. He went to his office with a much thicker file than a few days ago and closed the door. I was being blocked from any news about the case.

Around ten, we got into bed. I needed him to fall asleep so I could look in the file. I was curious, and my Schopenhauer studies were winding down. I had every intention of seducing him since I knew sleep after sex would induce the deepest sleep, but it was unnecessary; he was eager to roam my body with his hands. I opened my legs and coaxed him in. I thought it would go quickly as there was a fever in his eyes. I was wrong. Slow thrusts and strange whimpers from him took me by surprise. I might have said "don't stop" or "harder." I can't remember. I was so glad I wasn't in the den masturbating to long cum shots. When it was over, he went promptly to sleep, though he had placed his leg over mine, intertwining us. I waited, and once I was confident that he was starting an REM cycle, I carefully extricated myself from him and walked softly to his office. I turned on the light but did not see the file on his desk. I checked in the bottom drawer and saw it in a hanging file. I pulled it out carefully and opened it. There were several glossy photographs.

I found enlarged photos of the cross. I assumed it was the cross, since all the photos were close-ups and the wood was rippled with deep canyons. It was hard to determine if it was even wood with the magnification. The cross is a common symbol in Western civilization. So common, in fact, that one never really thinks of it. It was a method of execution by the Romans and it was the one chosen for Jesus. You see necklaces with crosses, earrings, books, and so many other products that one can easily stop thinking about its actual purpose. Lethal injection and the electric chair are methods of execution in the United States. Wouldn't it be strange to see people wearing syringes or electric chairs around their necks? The cross is also potent. It can make people cry despite the fact that it is nothing more than hunks of wood pounded together. The photographs highlighted the grain of the wood, and I wondered why there would be so many. I figured that it was because there was little other evidence to go on. The victim had not been identified. William would have told me. It would have been in the news. Tracking the wood, the screws and the nails holding it together was likely the only lead the Sheriff's Department had to solve the strange crime. Beneath the stack of photos was a white piece of paper. It stated the following:

Forensic Report on Cross

Wood: Cypress, likely originating in Louisiana

Screws and Nails: Pedestrian, available at most hardware stores

There are many species of Cypress in North America. The wood has been identified to be Louisiana Cypress and is prevalent in the Atchafalaya Basin in Louisiana, which is a swampy area larger than Florida's Everglades. It is 20 miles wide and 150 miles long. We can pinpoint no area more specific in that region.

Blood: The blood on the wood is being genetically typed. Results pending.

There was a multitude of other specifics on the form shared in a mind-numbing way with impeccable, scientific words. I straightened the file and placed it back in the filing cabinet. I hoped William wouldn't find its contents out of order. I went back to bed and wondered about a cross coming from Louisiana.

In the morning, William kissed me good-bye and I got dressed and went to the doctor. I explained to the nurse that I had thrown away my medications and needed refills, a new prescription.

"You threw the pills away?"

"Yep." I was looking at the wall behind her.

"Why?" The nurse was dressed in pink scrubs and she had baby blue Crocs on her feet. Her well-scrubbed face was devoid of makeup and her mass of ochre tinged blonde curls was piled on top of her round head.

"I didn't want to take them," I stated as her round eyes became confused.

"You couldn't just stop taking them without flushing them?"

She had a point.

"I was trying to make a point to myself."

"What was the point?" A naïve curiosity covered her face.

"I can't remember." It was true. In flushing the pills, I might have been symbolically flushing my life. I wasn't sure.

"Well, your insurance might not cover a new prescription. Of course, lithium is cheap and entirely affordable without insurance. I'm sure the doctor will want to speak with you before she writes a new prescription."

The nurse left and I was stuck in the exam room looking at fetus diagrams, a 3D model of female reproductive organs, and a humongous jar of tongue depressors. The doctor knocked and didn't wait for an answer. Her name was Dr. Morgan. She was knowledgeable and lovely and I hated her. Dr. Morgan was very abrupt, imperious, and kept reminding me that my biological clock was close to winding down. I didn't care. I wondered if she said that to the men. "Hey, soon you will be shooting blanks, better procreate. "Just because I had a uterus didn't mean I should use it.

"Are you seeing a therapist?" Dr. Morgan had her hands on her almost non-existent hips.

"Yep."

"Regularly?"

"Uh..."

"When was the last time you saw your therapist?" She wasn't letting up.

"Before my honey...vacation." I explained when that was.

"I'll write the prescription, but you need mental attention. I won't keep writing them without records from the therapist." She turned and walked out. Bye, bye.

The nurse kept me waiting another five minutes or so and then came back in with two written prescriptions. I checked them.

"Where's the prescription for Vyvanse?"

"You threw those away too?" She looked doubtful. I didn't throw them out. Who throws away speed? Vyvanse was an amphetamine similar to Adderall, except it was more stable and seemed to last longer for me. In addition to being bipolar, I also had ADHD. Some days I didn't take Vyvanse if I wanted to check out and be a groggy mess. Most days I tried to function, so speed was a requirement. Due to needing the drug in order to accomplish anything, I tried to stockpile pills. This explains why I was trying to get a new prescription.

"Yep."

"You know it's a controlled substance and you could be jailed?"

What's life without a little jail time? "I think I threw them out."

"What to check at home first?"

I was started to feel weird. "Sure, I'll check."

"See you in two weeks. Also, the doctor wants you to see your therapist within two weeks."

"Sure." Baby toys here I come.

I dropped the prescriptions off at the pharmacy. It only took thirty minutes to fill them as the pharmacy was slow. I read Schopenhauer on my phone. After picking up the prescriptions, there was nothing else to do. I went back home. The housekeeper was due the next day. Laundry was done. It was even folded. I stood in the middle of the house feeling out of place. I had options. Read, drink, porn. I figured I could do all three before William got home. For a fresh onlooker, it might have been strange watching me read Brecht, masturbate, and watch random porn, usually all at once, leading to a break involving long drinks of gin. It would seem chaotic, but like I said, I'm ADHD. After an hour or so and four or five orgasms, I decided to rest. That wasn't the record for an hour, but it wasn't really a competition. Or was it? In my alcohol and orgasm stupor, ideas wove together and what unfurled in my jellied brain was this – I would become a writer. Not a journalist, but a creative writer. I let the idea kick back in the brain chair for some time. Then I wondered what I would write. Was there a sealed locker of ideas that I could bash my way through? Or did I have a key? I held up *The Threepenny Opera*. Becht borrowed and refashioned the story from a 19th century English play. What's wrong with that? The best aspects of a piece of art are usually borrowed from somewhere else. Yes. I would write. I grabbed my porn notebook, went into the office, stared at a blank page, felt a moment of trepidation (pesky blank pages), swallowed it down, and began writing.

The Masturbator's Opera

Act 1

Peachum (to the audience): Something novel. That's what we crave. It is preferred to chase the novel and the different rather than sticking with reality. This is the truth: human desire is overflowing. A cup too full. It is best to have a glass of desire nearly empty than anywhere near half full. Two drops of desire is more than enough. It will allow you to want a partner and be hungry, slightly, for sex. That is manageable. Anything more and you are drowning. Chug, chug. You can't drink your own desire, silly. Spit it out. Do it. You'll get sick from your own desire. You can't live long on it. Eventually the desire rots in your gut, turning what is whole to mush. Every human knows the dangers of desire. They just don't know that they know. Humans are heartless. Discarding the heart is how they cope with desire. What do you do with your desire? Let's think. You are standing in a sweet shop and there is this wonderfully plump chocolate éclair. Your mouth fills up with saliva. You want it. Badly. You can't have it. You are trying to lose 5 pounds. The doctor you saw that morning says you have high blood pressure. You need to deny your desire. You walk away. You feel love for that éclair. You want to go back. Your friend asks if you want to get a sweet. No, you say, I hate chocolate, I hate cream, I hate sweets. You begin a sweetless life. There. The desire has been denied. Except you dream of sweets and that éclair, which now seems fatter. Obese with cream and chocolate. After a few months, you collapse in the grocery store and cry. You can't go on. You love the éclair.

Mrs. Peachum *(annoyed):* What does this have to do with me finding you masturbating in the kitchen sink?

Peachum: You weren't listening. Desire explains the masturbation. The kitchen sink was just the unfortunate reality.

Mrs. Peachum (angry): But I don't understand why. If you needed sex, you could have asked me.

Peachum: Sometimes we need to be alone in our desire. Plus, you don't arouse me any longer.

Mrs. Peachum: You better get to work before I murder you.

Peachum: Ah, my work. You mean where I outfit men to swindle people out of their money? I have many stockbrokers in my employ and I find new ones each day. Being a stockbroker is essentially about skimming off the work of others. I do nothing of any originality or importance. That's fine. No one should look for their life's purpose in work. Work is inhumane. It's stupid. Purpose is found in leisure. Purpose is found in love. Purpose is found in desire.

Act 2

Macheath (looking dapper): I'll murder you, Polly. I think I will.

Polly (looking lovely and greedy): It's not polite to tell a future wife you'll kill her on her wedding day.

Macheath: You're still here. I don't have any chains around you yet. Run away Polly, Polly.

Polly: I won't.

Macheath (looking at Polly with anger): You won't? That's because you are a greedy bitch. I didn't know it when I first saw your kind, honest face. Then I took money from my pocket, a hefty chunk, for your wedding dress and I saw it. Greed. You desire things like dresses, gloves, shoes. You want status. To be a proper wife. Your desire is for things, not people. You might be happier because of it but you will die empty. Things don't go to the grave.

Polly: I desire you.

Macheath: Do you now? You don't have to. I've other ways to meet my desire. I've women. Jenny Diver. Suky Tawdry. I have masturbation. I think I prefer masturbation. Less icky than clingy hands looking for money. Why can't a man's erection be appreciated and gazed up as nothing more than hardened desire? Why do women look at the cock and see money wrapped around the shaft. If I didn't have money, Polly, we wouldn't get married and you certainly wouldn't touch me. You liked my fine suit when you saw me. That's all.

Polly: We'll marry tomorrow. I don't care about the masturbation. Just don't do it in the kitchen sink.

Macheath: Do you masturbate?

Polly: No, that's silly. I've no desire that needs expunging.

Macheath: That's why it won't be sad when I murder you.

Polly: You know there is a song written about you? Mack the Knife.

Macheath: Hmmm...I'm a murderer with a song. Not unusual. They don't write songs about stockbrokers who golf on Tuesday mornings, play baseball on Saturdays, and take their awful kids to the park on Sundays. Nothing interesting there. A sad life, really. No desire other than for the women in the porn videos, but they only want them for a few minutes. Desire goes and they are back to doing whatever stockbrokers do. I should ask your father. Yes, I know the song. Comparing me to a shark. And then talking about all the blood. At least I wear gloves in the song. I hate blood. A murderer who hates blood. I don't murder because I want to soak my tired limbs in blood. I murder out of desire. I love watching the life ooze out of a body. It's so beautiful. Not the blood but the life in the blood that merges into the bedsheets. In the stains of death, there is an unfettered life. Bouncing out in the world, express ride to the universe. I like my song. Too jazzy for my taste. I would like it to be a dirge. A funeral song. I anticipate dying soon. I want people to stop and think and not dance all around.

Act 3

Suky Tawdry (to the audience): Yeah, Macheath is my customer. He leaves the money on the dresser. Crisp bills with the scent of danger. He tells me to count the bills. I do, and then stuff them in a drawer. Let's go, Mackie. Giddy up. He unfurls his cock. Size? Better than a stockbroker's but subpar for a murderer. The size of a cock says nothing about the size of the desire. Macheath has it deep within him. Wicked, bursting desire. He loves good bonking. Tasty lips. Flopping breasts. He doesn't get weak in desire. He doesn't stagger to the floor. Even in abandon, he's in control. His orgasms are clenched. Hard breathing as he squeezes my skin. A momentary fear riddling his face. And then release. The fear is interesting. He doesn't want to lose control. You have to do it if you want a fulfilling life. I'm telling you now. Let go in sex and you'll be a better person for it.

Do I masturbate? All whores do. While many of us get some pleasure from our work, don't forget it *is* work. You do not discover your life's purpose in work. We masturbate out of desire. It's not like it looks in porn. Masturbation is not so picturesque. You have to shake and flex your masturbation hand, repeatedly. Unless you come in a minute. That happens, especially if you have built up desire. Then there's the shuffling of images in your brain. Outwardly, this is expressed by eye clenching, head cocking, then opening and closing of the mouth, then pursed lips, then a ripple of frustration if it is taking too long, then the straining of the legs, then the changing in position. So much goes on and none of it cinematic. When the orgasm happens, it's wonderful because no one is around and you don't have to be self-conscious. Desire infecting your body. You lie in it. No rush to get out the door. Desire is a sickness and I want no part in a cure.

Act 4

Macheath (looking anxious): Your parents hate me, Polly. They've wanted me gone since they first met me. Why is that, Polly? Won't answer? I'm sitting in this jail cell and you won't tell me why your parents put in sweat and drippy, smelly hate to get me here. I think you owe me an answer. You're not my wife yet, but you owe me an answer.

Polly: Daddy thinks you're dangerous and mommy doesn't like your look.

Macheath: Your daddy is jealous and your mommy is desirous. You know she wants me, right?

Polly: I doubt that.

Macheath: When I get out of here, do you still want to get married?

Polly: I don't know. How you can get out? You're trapped.

Macheath: Escape is always possible. It's just often times you need a confluence of chance and intention.

Guard (looking bored): You're to be hanged now. Multiple murders, Mr. Mackie.

Macheath: I've known lots of desires. I took what I desired. My death won't be a sad thing for me. Satiating desire should be the main judge of a life. Not working, paying bills, or playing golf. You should ask a man. Did you desire greatly? If they say no, you know a demon cries somewhere and the man who desired so little should be swept into a universal dustbin. Now I desired greatly, and I shall be claimed as a great one. I guarantee that song, Mack the Knife, will outlive me. People a hundred years from now will listen to it and love it even though they have no idea what it means. I'll be a catchy song and my desire will be known.

Polly: Oh my, there are so many people here to watch you hang. These people want a show. Do they know a life is getting snuffed out?

Guard: They don't care. They just want a spectacle. They might say they are here to see justice served, but they don't care. They just want a spectacle. Watching someone swing gives them desire, momentarily. They can feel passionate about something. Get all worked up but not let down. A passionate life is not attained through another's misery and suffering. A passionate life is singular, personal and focuses only on your strengths and life. If your passion isn't all these things, then you only have hate, and there's no real desire in hate. Oh, look. The noose is hanging wrong and the scaffold is wobbly. Macheath, stand before the noose as I adjust it. Oh, damn. The noose is faulty.

Polly: Then you can't hang him.

Guard: Yes, I can. The law says I can.

Queen's Driver: Stop. Stop the hanging. I've news from the Queen. The Queen is releasing Macheath. She is dismissing all murder charges. Release Macheath now.

Guard: Suit yourself. The noose was all wrong anyhow.

Polly: And now the crowd is cheering because you are being released. That's very odd. Just a few moments ago, people were cheering because they wanted you dead.

Macheath: There has been a confluence of chance and intention. The majority of people are just sharks smelling blood droplets. They'll go anywhere the blood leads them. Let's get married.

Polly: You know, this doesn't really happen. Happy endings like this. Happy endings don't really happen.

Macheath: In movies they do.

Polly: That's illusion.

Macheath: You realize that we don't exist. You must realize that? We haven't left the paper.

The End

There was a shadow on my page. Was it Mackie? William was standing and looking down at the mad scribbles.

"I'm going to be a writer," I said. "I found my life's purpose. I just wrote a play. You can't read it, though. I don't want criticism thwarting my artistic endeavors."

"Can we go for a walk?" He stroked my shoulder. He looked pensive.

"We don't usually do that."

"Let's go outside. The temperature is mild and all the snow has burned off."

I put my shoes on and followed him outside. He was right about the snow. Most of it was gone. At the very tips of the mountains in the distance, there was snow. There was no snow on the ground. I didn't even put a jacket on. We started walking down the driveway and turned onto the main road where there was rarely a car passing by.

"What do you think of the writing?"

"If that's what you want…"

"I'm not fit for regular employment and writing would allow me to chase down all my interests."

"Then it sounds wonderful. I needed to talk to you about your parents and another issue that came up."

I was curious. "What did you find out?"

William picked up a marbled gray rock and threw it across the road. "The last known location of your mother was Louisiana. It was an apartment building that is no longer in existence. It was destroyed two years after she left you with Dobbs."

Mother, Marnie Blue, in Louisiana. A long time ago. I haven't really found her.

"She's dead?"

William scratched the side of his head. "I didn't say that. She may have changed her name, gotten a new Social Security number...she could be dead. She may also be alive living under an alias. I don't know."

"And my dad?"

"John Blue was getting checks from the Yaqui tribe up until about three years ago. The tribe has reported him as deceased. He was living in Phoenix at the same time as you. Also, the death was suspicious..."

"Suspicious?" I was confused.

"He committed suicide." William wouldn't look me in the eye.

"That's not suspicious." I wasn't surprised to hear that the father who left me when I was seven years old had been living in Phoenix and decided to take his own life. I was still curious, however, as to why he left mother and   me. Mother was horrible to him, but I thought he got along with me. He didn't really talk to me. Mother treated me like she hated me. Father never did that. I didn't feel like anything had been resolved by knowing about my parents. I still didn't know if my mother was alive or dead, and I didn't know why my father deserted me all those years ago. Who said knowledge could give you closure?

"There's something else."

William wrapped an arm around me and pulled me into him. "When you were found roaming the highway when you were nine, when you ran from Dobbs's house and were collected by the Sheriff and taken to the hospital, your DNA was typed. Standard procedure. Your DNA is now sitting in a database."

"Okay." His grip on my arm was fierce.

"We ran the DNA for the woman who was crucified. There was a familial match…with you. It is likely she is…was…your sister."

I tore from his arm. "What the hell?"

"The victim is probably your maternal sister."

"The girl on the cross? Slammed down at the entrance to Greer, where I used to live? The girl who's been to town and was fucking around? That's my mother's child?"

"Yes…"

"I had a sister?" I was incredulous.

"Seems so."

"And now she's dead." Tears were brimming in my eyes. It was unfair. I had wanted a sibling, a companion. I grew up so alone. Even as an adult, I would sometimes long for a sibling. Then I learned I had one, except she was dead, and worst of all I had looked at her on that cross with no feeling. No sympathy or tenderness. She was just an object wasting my time with her spectacle. "She's dead," I repeated. I felt wobbly on my legs.

"Let's go home. Lean on me."

Chapter 6

Oh, the Bible says this and the Bible says that. Mother wanted me to know she had read the Bible. I wish I had read it sooner, mother said. Can I read it? I asked. Get your fucking hands off. This isn't for you to read, she said. You have to be on the path to salvation to read the Bible and that's not you, she yelled. Besides, it doesn't matter completely what's in the Bible. What matters is how you act. If you act Christ-like, then you are blessed and special regardless if you know anything about theology. I'm focused on action, said mother. I yawned. The conversation was boring. You'll never be saved, she went on. I'm saved. I'm saved and can rest easily. You will have problems sleeping until the day you die because you won't let God into your heart. I had backed up to the hall. I didn't know what she was talking about. Are you listening to me, brat? You will never be a chosen one. No one will ever love you enough to sacrifice you. I went to my room and closed the door. Her words repeated in my head. No one will ever love me. No one will ever love me. There were many incidents with my parents that were painful. I was sure that prediction, no one will ever love me, was the most hurtful and harmful.

I had to do it. I had to visit Dobbs. I was an injured Ahab going after the white whale. The tormenting mystery of my mother. I didn't tell William my intention as he would have ruled against. His level of protection was appreciated, especially since I had never been protected, though it was becoming annoying and, I felt, sexist. I didn't want to say, "Hey you're being a sexist jerk. Dial it back. " I needed to be allowed to jeopardize myself and place myself in harm's way. I needed to be able to save myself. I and no one else was the key to my mental mending.

Mothers were horrible. No. Some mothers were horrible. Certain people just got lucky with sane mothers. The rest of us, however, were left to find warmth in the brutal winter of motherly neglect.

I was still finding it difficult to believe that mother had another child after me. She dropped me off at Dobbs's, with no intention of returning, and went out and got herself knocked up. Nice. I wondered if she was kinder to that child. I laughed. She couldn't have been. Somehow that child ended up crucified back in Greer.

After William told me the news, we went back home and I poured a gin and tonic. The warmth of liquor can resolve so much tension.

"Let's go out to eat." William had his coat on.

"Where?" I wasn't hungry. Just thirst for gin.

"Molly Butler's. This seems like a prime rib night."

Odd. To me it felt like a gin night. "Festive?"

"I didn't mean festive." William looked almost apologetic.

"Let's go." I downed my drink.

We were silent on the drive there, and I was glad there was no pressure to talk as I was swimming in my own thoughts. Molly's was half full so there was no wait for a table. I noted that the bar was busy, and I definitely wanted to be sitting there with drinks and mindless conversation. The waitress who sat us was quite young, likely no older that twenty-one, and had a luxurious mane of shiny black hair. She was pretty, but her young face was laden with powder and the opaque slicks of eyeliner. Her name tag read "Shoshana." She was quite courteous to William, and when she took our drink

orders she merely glanced at me but kept a delighted smile on him. I did not exist. I felt

like a geyser of heat, expelling annoyance and maybe jealousy. William wasn't being

anything more than polite. I'm not sure why I was jealous other than it seemed like

something I should be, as a new wife, to demonstrate my rapture of William. I was

jealous because in my usual mode, I needed to keep making a mess of my life, and

attacking William for flirting would piss him off.

"She seemed into you."

"Into me?" William looked confused.

"Like she wanted your dick in her mouth." I needed a martini, quickly.

William looked around to see if anybody overheard. "Did you forget we are in

public?"

"Did you forget she's a lot younger than you?"

William was about to say something but silenced himself when the waitress

arrived with my martini and his water. The waitress continued flirting, but William

wasn't responding. Not even with a glance. The waitress sauntered off with a dim frown.

"I'm going to forget this whole conversation. You got some bad news today. You

don't have to magnify trouble, Petra."

William folded his hands and gazed out the window where blackness, dotted

with only a few lights, reigned. The cars in the parking lot were distinct, but everything

else was just an inky mess. At my first meeting with William, I felt instantaneously

attracted. He felt the same about me. I don't know what that is. I don't think anyone does. What's involved in immediate attraction? Is it just physical attraction or is something else going on? I wasn't sure about my attraction until I looked him in his eyes and it was our eyes that latched onto each other, gazed at each other, for hours. If it had been purely physical, our eyes would have wandered all over each other's bodies. No. I could never be attracted to anyone for more than one night based on their ab structure alone. There was something more complex and mysterious going on with our quick attraction. As his wife, I should dedicate each day to figuring out what it is because if I do, we would have an unshakeable bond. I could remind him what the unnamed thing is each time I did or said something stupid. Maybe it was jealousy, the issue with the waitress. Since our bond was mysterious, it seemed like it was under threat from outsiders. That is what stabbed me with fear and panic in California when I met his family and friends but not his parents. None of those people knew what we had been through, and they were not in the room when we first met. They had no knowledge of our deep attraction or love and they would never know. For that reason, they were poised as an evil meant to derail us. We were Adam and Eve and everyone else in the world was the serpent.

I rubbed his leg under the table. He didn't look away from the window, though he seemed to relax and I thought I could see the corners of his mouth raise upward, just barely. There was a boy in high school that taught me the scary, icky feeling of jealousy. His name was Mason, I think. I'm bad with names and his name didn't suit him. I saw him playing in a school basketball game. He had blonde hair, but his skin was tan with little traces of pink.. He was the shortest boy on the team though at 5'8", he could still loom over most of the girls who edged near him for a drop of his attention. Mason was considered the "It" boy among the girls. I don't think any of the boys looked up to him.

His skills as a basketball player were only mediocre, he didn't play other sports, didn't

really talk about sports, and was only an average student in class. He did not have a

phenomenal intellect. Yet, I developed a crush on him for inexplicable reasons. Or

maybe not inexplicable. During the basketball game I had watched his body move in a

wholly male way, devoid of frippery, and he caught hold of the ball and passed it

elegantly but confidently. It was not athletic prowess that was responsible for the crush.

It was that his body movements seemed to be making a personal statement, offering a

glimpse into his personality. He was male, not without appreciation of females, and even

if both of those characteristics were gone he would still have a solid sense of self. When I

approached him after the game, I realized there was more than just his body from a

distance that attracted me. The undeniable shivery sparkle in his lagoon-colored eyes

suggested amusement, a bite of sarcasm, and the rarity of happiness. I was hooked even

though I knew I wasn't his type. The girls he dated were altogether different from me.

None were overly studious, or moody, or brutal, or inclined towards self-loathing. The

fact that he couldn't like my personality should have been grounds for me not liking

him. He might have been a new way for me to demonstrate my self-hatred. I followed

him around campus and got one of my classes switched to a class he was in. I watched

him for an hour flirting with three of the girls in the class and only occasionally glancing

at me. A month later he got a serious girlfriend and was frequently seen kissing her, but

not with youthful pecks or youthful ardor. He kissed her in a way that seemed deeper,

intense, hungry, but nevertheless restrained because he might be consumed in the

moment if he wasn't careful. When I saw that kiss, only one thing entered my mind. He

loved her. I went to the bathroom and kicked the wall until a school worker came in and

dragged me to the office. I was written up for school vandalism. The Vice Principal asked me why I was kicking the wall and I told him it was because of love. He thought I was being a jerk and sent me to detention for the rest of the day.

The next day I saw his girlfriend sitting alone at a library table. She was studying and alternately plaiting her long auburn hair. I hated her. I willed her to die. She made me sick. To continue going to school knowing she existed was too much to withstand. I thought of ways to get rid of her. Push her into oncoming traffic. Trip her and hope she splits her head open. Take a hammer and bash her head in. There were a lot of options and I didn't need to make a decision. My group home had me placed in a different group home due to my behavior issues. I had a new high school and there were no boys that captured my imagination. My obsession with Mason diminished and I was saved from committing an awful crime. No. I was not really jealous of the waitress. And William now had his eyes on me and was smiling. My foot was meandering very far up his thigh, which was probably an inappropriate thing to do to the Sheriff in a public area. William looked more intensely interesting than that silly Mason boy. William's every movement seemed to have some kind of statement that I needed to decipher and read.

The prime rib at Molly's was actually superb and I, untypically, ate everything on my plate while managing to drink two more martinis. William didn't quite manage to finish his food and that was strange. I figured it was the case. He didn't look pensive though. He was watching me eat with a happy look that I didn't acknowledge because I was caught up in hunger.

As we exited the restaurant, I saw Loose sitting at the bar talking to a middle-aged woman with corkscrew curls and an AC/DC shirt. I headed over to him.

"Where are you going?" William sounded a trifle annoyed.

I tapped Loose on the back. "I need to talk to you about Lotte Lenya."

Loose swiveled around and then looked at William approaching. "Is this an official Sheriff Department talk?"

"I don't know, is it?" I glanced at William who was now standing next to me.

"What's this about?" William asked.

"Your wife wants to ask me more questions about your victim." Loose seemed neither annoyed nor pleased.

"Not here." William's voice was curt and professional. "You can come down to the station tomorrow if you wish to make a statement."

"I don't. I don't think I know anything at all that could be helpful. All I really had was her name."

"Petra told me and the name is likely false." William was pulling on my arm.

"Wait. Loose, what was she like?" I really just wanted to know, in any way I could, what my sister was like.

"A feral cat."

"You said that. Anything else?"

"I was really drunk, Petra."

"Can you give me something?"

Loose closed his eyes for a moment and then touched my arm. "She had really sad eyes like you, Petra."

"Let's go." William grabbed my arms and pushed me towards the door.

"She said she also knew love. I think that's what she said. Yeah, she knew love. With her sad eyes I guess it went away." Loose swiveled back to the bar and continued his conversation with the woman next to him who had been slowly drinking her beer the whole time.

"Stop it." I yelled at William.

"Keep your voice down." He guided me into the passenger side of the car and had to push me as I wouldn't bend my body.

"Are you okay?" He was pulling the seatbelt around me to fasten it. He had this weird thing of obsessing over my seatbelts.

"I just wanted to know about her."

"I know. I know." He had his nose pressed up against my ear. I could feel his breath down my neck. He smelled faintly of roasted butter. I moved so I could kiss him. His lips and tongue were sharply salty and meat rich. Our meal tasted even better in his mouth.

"I just wanted to know about her." I was doing small kisses across his face.

"I know. I don't want you getting depressed or unstable."

"I started the medications again. I'm fine."

He stood up and smoothed my hair. "I feel like you're still hiding something from me."

I swallowed and made a decision. "I may have acquired a recent addiction to porn."

I heard William sigh. "I already knew that."

"What? How did you know?" I felt a vibe of panic.

"Never mind how I know."

"I do mind. How do you know? Have you been snooping on my computer?"

"I can hear you. I can hear the porn and I can hear you." He didn't look upset.

"You didn't answer the question."

"About the computer? Yes, I have been on your computer." He had placed his hand on the car so he could lean closer to me in the car seat. "It was easy enough figuring out your password was William."

I was losing it. I was angry and I felt violated. "Why would you do that?"

"I was worried about you and I knew something was going on. I saw your notebook on our last day in California. A list of every conceivable sex act. You could only have gotten that from porn. Are you going to do something self-destructive now? Something hurtful to me?"

I was pouting. "You were policing me."

"No, not at all. I was just learning about you to prevent anything unfortunate from happening. I had no intention to make you stop."

"You shouldn't have," I insisted half-heartedly. William and I were intimate – sexually and mentally. It seemed stupid to have even made it a secret from him. I should have just told him. He wouldn't have made me stop. That was true.

"I'm curious as to why it began when we got married."

I shrugged my shoulders. "I just…

"What?"

"Feel unending desire and it doesn't feel good. It's a torment. It might be that I stopped taking my meds and it hasn't been enough time in restarting them. But…that's why I don't like the meds. It feels like the pills are burying something to make me indifferent to it. It seems dishonest."

William was quiet a second and then closed the car door. I watched him walk around to the driver's side. He got in, turned on the ignition, and then fastened his seatbelt. But he didn't drive. He exhaled some breath.

"Am I meeting your needs…sexually?"

I chuckled. "It has nothing to do with you. It's just something I always felt. You haven't made the longing for something go away. No. But you haven't made it worse. Actually, I would say you've improved it. I'm better with you. I'm sure this isn't what you want to hear." I paused to think. "Am I meeting your needs? I don't yet understand your sexuality."

"My sexuality is not even close to the complexity of yours."

"You didn't answer the first question."

William tapped his fingers on the steering wheel. "You are everything I ever wanted and you exceed my needs. Isn't it obvious?" His glance was quizzical.

"I'm not very good at reading people. Be sure to let me know if you need more of...whatever. I could easily seduce you every time you walk through the door. You generally don't look in the mood though. You don't have the look until we are behind our bedroom door. I think you are rigid as to time and place of sex."

William left the parking lot and drove down Main Street to the highway. He was quiet and so was I. The conversation did not go well.

"I'm not rigid. I'm just not addicted to sex."

"Like me."

"It's reasonable that you would develop a sex addiction given your childhood history of sex abuse."

I thought for a few seconds. "I don't think it is a true sex addiction. It gets worse when I'm manic and nearly goes away when I am severely depressed. Bipolar is partly responsible for my so called addiction. I'm not making it up. I spoke to my therapist about it."

"Okay. We won't call it an addiction. We'll call it hypersexuality. I don't want sex all the time because I am not hypersexual."

"Well, that sucks for you. The all-consuming desire is really striking and lovely."

"Are you being sarcastic?"

"Partially. Are you sure you don't want more sex? It might help with my, you know, hypersexuality."

"I could..." He put his hand on my leg.

"Never mind."

"Why?" His hand went further up my leg.

"Too late. I heard doubtful pondering."

"That's crazy. I want you. I never considered...having such an active sex life."

"Now you have me." I moved his hand to my unfortunately clothed vagina.

"I do, and if it delays porn watching, all the better."

"What's your issue with porn?" I was twisting his arm to attempt to get his fingers in the right position. I needed pressure on my endlessly delightful clitoris.

"I don't want any of those women. It's imperfect and sad jerking off to a woman you wouldn't even want to talk to, much less make love to."

His index finger was finally pressing the right spot. I moved forward into his hand and moaned. A tiny moan. I felt the car swerve.

"You can't do that while I'm driving." He started to move his hand away.

"No, keep your hand there."

"I'm going to kill us both." He let his hand rest on my leg.

I sat back and closed my eyes and focused on the sensation of his hand on my thigh. We arrived home safely and accident free. William took my hand to lead me to the bedroom but I pulled away.

"Not the bedroom," I said. "Here, the living room. Don't argue."

I threw my shoes across the room and then began discarding my clothes. William stood watching with an incandescent desire suffusing his face.

"You need to take off your clothes too. Now."

He looked self-conscious as he took off his shirt. He hesitated at his pants. I laughed.

"I know what you look like. Why so shy?"

"Being gazed on is a little uncomfortable."

"Holy shit. That's what you do to me, all the time. That's what men do to women, all the time."

"Alright." He slowly took off the rest of his clothes and I did what he did not like. I gazed. Openly, ardently, and voraciously. And he recognized the depth of my desire because his erection, which had fallen in his self-consciousness, was now fully engorged. I went up to him and grabbed hold his penis and moved my hand and listened intently to the change in his breath. His jaw tightened. He was biting back hunger.

"You can do anything you want to me," I breathed. He pulled me down onto the carpet, kissed my inner thighs and then put the right amount of pressure on my clitoris that he couldn't do in the car. I could have come in the first minute but I decided to take advantage of his ardor and prolonged my pleasure.

Lotte Lenya – Letter #2

My heart was dreary and teary. I kept thinking of Macheath, lying mutilated in that cramped and damp wooden shack on the swamp. If I thought of the blood and his wound I vomited. All stomach contents rushed up and out. I began thinking of him as I knew him. I thought of the neatness of his clothes, the pleased look in his milk chocolate-colored eyes when I wrote an essay he liked, the flatness of his stomach when he was stretched out in my bed, that musky vanilla smell that was always on his body, the deepened laugh lines that rippled into more lines when he smiled in delight, the way he twisted his hand into my hair when we made love, and that momentary look of uneasy abandon when he climaxed. My grief was unending and I could barely wash myself for weeks. I lost fifteen pounds in a month. Mother was annoyed.

"What's wrong with you?"

I didn't answer. I had no interest in talking to her any longer. She pulled the cover back.

"I didn't know you would react this way. What's wrong with you?"

I sobbed and shook and mother dropped the blanket.

"Oh," she said. "You were in love with him. I didn't know you loved each other."

My sobbing became full of rage. "Get out." I had never yelled at her before.

"I'm your mother." She had her hands on her hips.

"Kill me." I knew what needed to be done. "Kill me. Kill me or I will kill myself."

Mother looked alarmed. "I won't." She left, and then a woman around thirty years old began sitting in my bedroom every day. She usually read a magazine or stared out the window. She followed me to the bathroom and tried to force food on me. In the evening, a new sitter came and she was focused on knitting. I wanted to stab both of them. I wanted to be alone. I started playing music on my phone and kept the ear buds in. I played "The Rose" by Bette Midler at least a thousand times in a few days. The song did not make me feel better.

"I can't take this." I put my shoes on and went outside. The day sitter questioned me and I said I needed air. She followed my trip around the neighborhood. I cried as I walked.

"What made him special?" the day sitter inquired.

"Everything," I answered. "He was sweet, kind, intelligent, gentle, handsome…I've run out of things. There's more though. A lot more."

"What was your connection?" she pressed.

I thought about that. "We were intellectually and sexually intimate. I can't think of anything better. It's the mind-body connection people talk about. I was lucky enough to find it at a young age. We loved each other and now it is gone. I don't know what to do."

"You get hard." The day sitter was staring at a cypress tree.

"Hard as wood?"

"Harder than that. Strive for steel."

"I don't think so. It's not my nature." There was a distinct break in my heart that had begun the moment I saw Macheath laid out on the bed and it had continued. I wished it would just finish the process. I wished it would snap and leave me alone already.

"It will have to be your nature. If you don't become hard, then everything you do, from this moment on, will take something from you and you will leave with less than you came with. It is better to go against your nature than to lose yourself." The day sitter brushed her blonde bangs from her eyes and slowed her walking. For the first time, I noticed she was lean, muscular and carried herself with measured confidence. She was the kind of person who did not want to draw attention to herself.

"What am I doing from this moment on?"

"Your mother will tell you." She touched my arm to increase the pace, but I responded by stopping altogether.

"Tell me. You can tell me because you brought it up."

The day sitter's face had that stony sheen of indifference. "You will be managing the flow of girls into your mother's brothels and negotiating the sale to buyers throughout the US. That will entail developing and maintaining good relationships with many European suppliers and good communication skills for the other buyers."

I stared at her as if she was speaking a foreign language. And then I started laughing loudly and hoped the neighbors would come out of their expensive, safe homes.

"You need to stop." The day sitter gripped my arm and led me further down the street.

"Let go of me, you evil thing." I was now chuckling.

When we were under the shade of a Witch Hazel tree she let go of me.

"You're crazy," I voiced.

"It's the truth."

"Why would she give me a sheltered upbringing and a supremely intellectual education, only to expect me to debase myself and communicate with heathens?"

"The men, mostly men, involved in sex trafficking are not what you may think. Many respond well to strong intellects and feel better doing business with someone who has read *The Brothers Karamazov* rather than someone who has never even heard of the book. You mother made a good decision in your education."

"That's horrible. Educated criminals insisting on dealing with other educated criminals." I shivered, despite the fact that it was balmy.

"It's how it is."

"And criminal. It's all criminal."

"Few would suspect a young woman like yourself. Also, your business contacts would trust you."

"And take advantage of me." A strange complacency was settling in my bones. All I had ever known was my mother, my home, and Macheath. With his death, I was left with an even narrower world. I wanted to go to college except I did not take the SAT, had no one to write me a recommendation, and I wasn't sure I met all the schooling requirements. My education, while excellent, would have been more typical for someone around the turn of the 19th century. It stranded me in the swamp with mother. I realized had no choice but to comply with her wishes regarding my future.

"Your mother will train you." The day sitter took a few steps to encourage me to walk. I headed back home and went into the study for the first time in weeks. My fingers touched the spine of every book as I thought of Macheath and the paradise we had created for ourselves. I desperately wanted that refuge back, but it was lost. Vivid memories that had the shocking veneer of being surreal were giving me the distance I needed to move on.

Over the next year, mother trained me in the hard facts of sex trafficking. She was entirely objective about it. She said nothing against it or for it. It was a reality that she was sharing, and opinions would not change that reality. In dealing with the contacts, she never became vulgar or stopped being religious. She instructed me to remain who I was: a classically educated, relatively inexperienced woman from the Bayou who had seen little of the world.

"Isn't it dangerous to be myself? I've no defenses."

"That's why you have bodyguards." I had been assigned two guards who were imposing, simmering with violence, and graced with blank faces. "You might also want to increase your experience of the world. You need to go beyond Macheath." She got into her car and closed the door. The driver lowered the window. "You don't need to sneak around anymore. You're a grown woman and you have your own car and driver. You have my blessing."

That was humorous. A blessing for sex. I had no intention of pursuing any type of relationship. I was a little too young to say I was done. I obviously was not. My sex life had just begun with Macheath. Sometimes I wondered how long we would have been together. Forever was not a word I used, even with Macheath. Even so, we could have gone on for years and years,   fueled by our distinctive love.

I told the driver to take me to a coffee house across town where I could read and think. The house now felt confining, and frequent departures are what made it bearable. I ordered a decaf coffee, as it was nearing six in the evening, and opened my book. I can't remember the title and it likely wasn't literature. I had been making an effort to be less rarefied and had started reading books that were mainstream. I didn't enjoy them; however, they did help me deal with the daily madness and brutality that defined my life.

"Your nose is always in a book."

I looked up and my mother's former bodyguard, one of the men who killed Macheath, was looming over me. I didn't know his name.

"Can I sit?" He pointed to the tufted chair next to me.

I shrugged. "I don't own the chair."

"I thought it polite to ask before I encroached on your space." He was dressed in black with a designer t-shirt, slacks, and dress shoes. He could have gone to a gallery opening or been a bouncer at a high-end strip club.

"That's an interesting statement from you."

"Why is that?" He was looking at me with a mischievous smile.

"I won't answer that. Why are you here?"

"I had business a few doors down. When I walked passed, I saw you."

"I haven't seen you in a while." I finally closed my book.

"I was out of the country. I'm back as your mother's second in command. You'll start seeing me." He sounded so professional and yet so pedestrian. He spoke as if he was talking about getting a promotion at an investment bank instead of an illegal sex trafficking business.

"Wonderful," I said, and picked up my book.

"You don't mean that." He was still grinning.

"Your right, I don't." I opened the book in hopes he would leave.

"Your mother told me to find you and seduce you." He was no longer smiling.

"Why would she want you to seduce me?" I didn't put anything past my mother.

"I'm sure you could figure it out."

"I don't want to sleep with you." No way.

"We wouldn't be sleeping." He leaned back in the chair with annoying confidence.

"We would be..." I was wondering about the best word for the situation and the location.

"Say it."

"I won't."

"And that's why you need to be seduced. You can't even say fuck."

I refused to leave with him. Over the next two weeks, I saw him at several meetings and each time, after the meeting ended, he would remind me that we were supposed to fuck. His word. The more I saw him, the more I began to wonder what it might be like to have sex with him. He was the opposite of Macheath, not just in intellect, but also in physique. Macheath had a slender body strengthened by a diet of poetry and irony. Matthew, the name my mother told me after I kept calling him the former bodyguard, was over six feet, muscular, and spoke with no vacillation or embarrassment. He never bowed his head or made a sidelong glance. I wondered how that would translate sexually. I vowed not to find out. A week later, mother went away for an extended trip, and Matthew and I were in charge of business meetings and decisions. We were in downtown New Orleans, and he said there were documents I needed to sign so he could give them to the lawyers. I knew it was a ploy but I played along. I knew he wouldn't press me if I screamed rape. That would be bad for his career. He lived at the top of a skyscraper. It wasn't a penthouse or the very top. He was near the top and on a floor with many others who could afford a piece of the New Orleans skyline. The loft was modern, and decorated almost entirely in white and brushed silver with a stainless steel kitchen. It was also flooded with light, even at night, due to the track lighting. I signed the forms and waited, as I expected him to break out whatever moves he had for convincing women to have sex with him. He did nothing, and then told me I could go when he saw I didn't move.

"You're not going to try?" I was a little offended.

He frowned. "You want me to try?"

The truth was that I was sexually frustrated, and most days I wanted to weep tears of annoyance and exasperation. I might as well claim my sexuality, stamp it as owned. The only thing that did not make me desperate was my youth. Youth, sometimes mistakenly, believe they have years and years ahead to achieve what they desire and need.

"I want you to try." I didn't want attempts at trying. I weaved my way through his luxurious and oddly stringent loft until I found his bedroom, thankfully free of irritating light, and undressed slowly - not because I was being seductive, but because I was building my commitment to the endeavor. Matthew stood watching me, full gaze and minus the blaze of kindness that had been on Macheath's face. He lifted me up and threw me onto the bed like he was chucking a stuffed animal. I was scared and excited at the same time. He then took his clothes off and I only glanced at him as hot embarrassment pulsed at my cheeks.

"Look at me." He grabbed me by my legs. "Look." I still couldn't and I tried squirming out his grasp. "It's your right to gaze. I've been looking at you this whole time."

I stopped moving and let my eyes fall from his head, down his face that looked even more brutal, his solid chest, his stomach with a few hairs down the middle, his penis that looked quite different from Macheath's in size, coloring, and shape, and the tops of his thighs that I could see from lying down in bed. I looked, but did I see? I went to his eyes and saw danger, a lack of tenderness, cruelty, eagerness, hunger, and a glint of adventure.

"You killed the love of my life." I wanted him to know I had not forgotten.

"I'm sorry." He crawled onto the bed and kissed my knee as his hand moved upwards across my body. When he cupped my breast he came up and kissed the other nipple. This was almost like having sex with Macheath and I closed my eyes and thought of him. It went on for more blissful seconds, possibly a minute, and then he slapped me.

"Hey…" I was annoyed he interrupted my thoughts, and the slap was hard and stinging.

"Stop dreaming about your boyfriend." His face was very near mine and he seemed displeased. He made no indication of wanting to kiss me. He held down both my arms and so roughly entered me that I screamed out of surprise and some pain. My instinct was to think I was being raped, except the sensations of his fucking were making me delirious. I went on screaming. I was delighting in the brutality. And that's all I needed to leave Macheath behind me, feel less sorry for myself, and more fully accept the role I was playing in sex trafficking. Unconfined lust helps you learn a truth about the world. Desire makes you reckless and cruelty is sometimes desirable.

Chapter 7

When Dobbs first came to our home, mother was excited. She placed a plate of cookies out for him. I never got a plate of cookies. Mother also brought out the Bible. Dobbs entered like he was the landlord and his eyes rested on me like I was a doll to be shelved, cradled or broken. He shifted his attention back to mother. She had on a long ruby-colored skirt and a white blouse. She was barefoot and her red hair was loose and hanging past her waist. She had flame tresses and each strand seemed alight with energy. Dobbs focused his attention on mother, and they spoke for some time about the Bible. Then Dobbs wanted her to pray with him. Mother looked pleased and bowed her head, but then he insisted on praying with no clothes on. I pray as I was born. Mother looked confused and fearful, but only momentarily. She got hard. They went to her bedroom and I wanted to ignore them, except I couldn't. I wanted to know what was going on in that room. I tiptoed over to the door and leaned my ear onto the cold, beige paint. I heard whacks and thunks and possibly my mother whimpering. I also heard whispering, fast and low, like secret retching. Pained and then relief. Our father. Heaven. Blah. Blah. Blah. Strange praying. Strange indeed.

Despite my realization that William and I had a bond beyond sex, and that I had shared, on several occasions, truths that had been manipulating my life, I still decided not to tell him about visiting Dobbs. I was still not comfortable with my reality, my past, my curse. I need to muck through the shit alone. When William left for work, I got dressed in a navy blue dress and heels, which was uncharacteristic. I was dressed very grownup with a strong suggestion that I had become successful in life. The reason for my choice of clothes was not mysterious. I wanted the man who sexually abused me as a child to know that I , had survived, and that his actions did not destroy me. I had last seen Dobbs in December, and, in my characteristic way, had not dealt with the emotions of seeing my abuser as my mind instantly began solidifying into numbness. I wasn't sure how I would react this time. I hoped I could remain calm, as I needed answers to my questions regarding my mother.

Dobbs was in a nursing home. In December, he was ill and nearing death, but through some kind of action by a possibly psychopathic God, Dobbs lived and improved. He had improved enough for a nursing home and was placed in one in Show Low.

I made the drive to the facility in silence. I refused to turn the stereo on, as I needed to focus on keeping my breath even. Dobbs couldn't hurt me. He couldn't hurt me. I repeated that to myself. Over and over. My breath still clogged my throat like old, used motor oil.

The nursing home was a squat building with no adornment. It was pure function. Nothing more or less. It was stucco, dark ivory paint, a slightly sloping roof, and a bland sign. Home of the Aged. The lobby was lilac and snowy white. There were awful pictures of sunsets and flowering trees in thin frames.

"Can I help you?"

The nurse at the desk appeared to be in her sixties with an angular body. You might have been able to file a nail on her hip bone. Her voice was curt and seemed to say that she had too much to do rather than talk to me.

"I'm here to see Mr. Dobbs." My throat was scratchy.

"You are? He doesn't get visitors." The nurse looked suddenly alight with curiosity. Her voice now said she had time to talk. "Who are you?"

"A visitor."

The nurse clicked a pen. Click. Click. "You'll have to provide your name." She pushed a book towards me. A visitor's log. I wrote my name, Petra Blue. I had not taken William's last name of Armor. Dobbs would know me as Petra Blue.

"You came during nap time. I can show you to the Day Room. You can wait there. Nap ends in about twenty minutes. I'll make sure one of the staff brings Dobbs in. He usually sits in the Day Room for most of the day."

She came around the nurse's station and I followed her down a short hallway that opened into a sprawling room ensconced in more lilac and white. There were pictures of old-fashioned clowns. No, Bozos. Ominous, Depression era clowns with faces that looked more sad than happy. One was holding a wilting flower with broken petals. I sat by the window. "It won't be long." She walked away and I noted again how painfully skinny she was.

The chair I was sitting in was pale lilac and well cushioned, but wrapped in faux leather. It looked cheap and industrial. It could see scratch marks on either side of the chair. I wondered about that, but didn't consider it for long as the idea of having to wait, being suspended in the suspense, was twisting my stomach. I leaned back and looked out the window. It was a fittingly dreary day. A winter sky out of place in the spring weather. I thought of waiting and what it meant to wait. Waiting was the expectation of something to come, something that may never come. Most of us wait our whole lives, and some of us figure out how not to wait for anything, to live each moment as if it were whole. I wasn't one of those people. I couldn't live in the moment because I was deficient. I needed something, constantly, and to give in to the moment meant to accept the need.

Sometimes we wait thinking we need one thing but really need another. When World War II started, Brecht made a run for it. He went from country to country and eventually found his way to Los Angeles in 1941. LA was home to a large German émigré community as well as other European expats. Nearly all wanted to cash in on the motion picture business. Brecht barely spoke English, but that didn't stop him from pitching movie outlines to studio execs. It was a rough existence for Brecht. Most people in LA had no clue who the surly German man was. Threepenny Opera? Who cares? Brecht in Europe had his precious reputation. Brecht in LA had *staccato* English. He had a few contacts – Peter Lorre and Fritz Lang. Lang understood who Brecht was and helped him craft something the studios would like. "Ask yourself one thing," Lang said "Will people buy it?" That was a new question for Brecht. He usually just created from an ideological idea. He never wondered if people might actually like what he produced.

Brecht could not warm to LA. He lobbed insults at Salk Viertel's salon in Santa Monica, like "LA shrivels up the brains of real writers." Thomas Mann took offense and declared Brecht awful. Poor Brecht. He had no friends in sunny California. His buddy Weill showed up in LA, but only briefly. Hi, there old boy, said Weill. You look dirty, unshaven, and, might I say, pathetic. You are easier to deal with though. A defeated Brecht is much easier to deal with. Brecht got angry at Weill. I just wait, he said. I wait around all day. I'm waiting for a call from the studios. Weill considered this. You should write scripts in the middle of the waiting. If that's what you are waiting for. Brecht shrugged. What else would I be waiting for? Weill knew his friend was an ardent Marxist and he was in a country without a strong whiff of that ideology. Weill figured Brecht might be waiting for a revolution in a capitalistic society, in a capitalistic city where money, not dreams and ideas, makes the world turn. Hollywood wasn't about ideology. It was the inoculation for ideology. Brecht grew sulky and wanted to be alone with his typewriter, his radio, his bed. Weill left and Brecht moped and kicked the carpet. He went to his balcony and could see the LA basin twinkling below him. His rented home was in the hills, and if he could stop being so Brechtian, he might have enjoyed the beauty of where he was living and the honeyed light that shone most days of the year. He couldn't, though. He was waiting. Not for a phone call from a studio, not for a revolution or ideological warmth. Something different. Something that had always been there, poking his intestines like gas. Fame and intellectualism only obscured and quieted the annoyance. He was waiting, and in that waiting was the self, the self he suppressed, the self that was unhappy with ideology. All great thinkers have longing, desire, and some darker energy I cannot name. Brecht was waiting for the day when all would go away. He wanted the trio to crawl off and die miserably. In LA, the trio was irritating. Go away. If only he had a friend to consume the hours with. Alone with your thoughts, there were only feelings and gloom.

I stretched my arms as my mind lingered on Brecht standing, fully clothed, on a sunny Malibu shore looking for a Marxist. I heard voices and turned to see a few elderly women hobble into the room with canes and walkers. They were chatting, and only one acknowledged me. The women sat at a table where there was a half-finished puzzle. I watched as more old people came in. There was a rotund elderly man who limped and took his seat in the corner. He had a James Patterson novel in his hand. Light reading as you near death. Then, from the corner of my eye, I saw a glint of silver as a wheelchair rounded the doorframe and entered the spacious room with the tall windows overlooking a humdrum parking lot. The wheelchair was heading towards me and I assumed that the figure stuffed in it was Dobbs. He had the appearance of a gutted corpse, like his organs were stored in jars and all that was left was a crusty shell. He looked pained and glum, and I detected glee in those thin, cracked lips and skeletal face. It may have been only a strong echo of glee bouncing across the chasm of his voided soul, but it was glee lifting his sagging face as he saw me sitting in that putrid lilac chair. I did not get up. Dobbs was wrapped in layers of white – white shirt, white robe, and a white sheet that ensconced his cadaverous figure. The nurse parked his wheelchair in front of the window and took off, like she was excited to be done with the toxic man swaddled like a baby. Dobbs said nothing and didn't really look at me. He could detect and likely smell my presence.

Dobbs and I had an interesting history. When my mother dropped me off at his house and disappeared, he began sexually abusing me. I was getting queasy remembering his penis and thinking, unfortunately, how curled up and useless his must now be. I stared out the window and pretended to be fascinated with a pine tree. I got pissed at myself. I did not go to Dobbs to look at the scenery. I wanted to know things.

"Marnie Blue. Tell me about her." I wasn't sure Dobbs would even remember my mother's name.

"Nothing to tell. Don't care to remember those days." I had expected a long silence and a tiny, dry voice. What I got was a prompt response and a fully present voice that was clear and chilling. The voice from long ago.

"You remember me?"

"Oh, yes. Petra Blue. I had so much fun with you."

My head almost exploded with rage. I wanted to walk away. I wanted to run. I didn't think my legs would work.

"Why did my mother give me to you?"

Dobbs's creepy fingers flexed and moved like spider legs on the wheelchair arms. "I asked her to. Give me the riches of your home and I will give thee a blessing for personal riches."

I was quiet and thought I could hear something breaking. I wondered if it was in me. It was astonishing how much damage Dobbs could do in mere seconds.

"What did she want?"

Dobbs slyly looked at me. "Want?"

"What did my mother want?" I spoke very slowly.

He waved his hand. "Ack. What every woman wants. She wanted pretty, pretty things. Money. That woman wanted money. It's unholy to want so much money. You will do evil things if you want money that badly."

I laughed sharply. "You did evil things and wanted no money."

Dobbs gave me another sly glance and gripped his wheelchair. He remained silent until the arrival of a van in the parking lot piqued his interest.

"Ah, looks like we will be getting some ice cream for dinner."

I looked out the window and saw a Blue Bell Ice Cream delivery truck pull up near the front entrance.

"He needs to go to the side where the cafeteria is. I do hope he is able to deliver the ice cream. I would love a nice bowl of cookies n' cream. Do you like ice cream, Petra?"

"Yes, but I prefer strawberry."

"There is a creaminess to strawberry."

If Andre Breton were alive, I would have had to write to him and advise him that all the surrealist moments he chronicled in his books and the surrealist paintings he discussed with Magritte and Dali were shit. Melting clocks. Nice one Dali. But do you think you could get weirder? Dali should have painted me and Dobbs. A woman, thirty-five, in a blue dress discussing ice cream with a decrepit man who also sexually abused her. He could call it *Ice Cream Fuck*.

"What did you give my mother so she could get money?"

"I don't remember." He sunk a little deeper into the wheelchair.

"You do remember." I was getting furious. Again.

"What does it matter?" Oh. Petulance. The tone of voice of a nine year old. We never really grow up.

"The evil you did to me means you owe me answers."

"It wasn't evil."

If I were a cartoon, my jaw would have dropped to the floor. "It was and why would you think otherwise?"

"Well, well, well. You weren't always miserable when we played."

If only I had a baseball bat. I was starting to see that maybe I should have invited William. I grabbed the sheet wrapped around Dobbs and started pulling on it. His whole body moved with the direction of the sheet, causing the wheelchair to begin tipping. One of the ladies at the puzzle table shrieked, so I let go of the sheet. The wheelchair released and slammed back down onto the floor, causing Dobbs to baby bounce. Dobbs was expressionless the whole time. It crossed my mind that he may have wanted me to kill him.

"You almost made me kill you. You never took a piece of me, but you almost made me commit a crime just now. You would have taken a piece today. So we're clear. You never took a piece of me. Your abuse changed my direction. You didn't crush me. Humans are more flexible than that. We think things break us – trauma and love. Isn't that what we say? You broke my heart. The heart didn't break, it just changed direction. We don't say trauma broke our heart. It's easy to imagine it breaking our bodies. Even so, it still changes our direction. I didn't do so well after I ran from your prison. I'm still not well. I'm better, though not well. Of course, I always feel like I'm one step away from completely fucking everything up. That's a lot of pressure. I found out I have a sister. The problem is that she is a murder victim. I'll never know anything about her. My father is dead. My mother...presumably alive. I didn't like her when I was a child. I can't imagine I'd like her now. But I need to know about her. I need answers, Dobbs. I don't need your insolence and further abuse. Do you understand that you changed my life for the worst? The worst. And for most of my life, I thought I was a bad person. Probably still do. I know you are a bad person. You and your evil soiled me. I need answers, Dobbs."

I hooked my hair behind my ears and breathed, in and out, to try and steady myself. My hands were shaking and, despite the anger, I felt a rush of deep weariness. I wondered if there was a spare bed.

"I gave her a name."

"What did you say?"

"I gave your mother a name. She wanted to be rich. So I gave her a name. She gave you to me in return."

I sniffed and swallowed because my throat felt constricted. "What was the name?"

"Tyson Yeager."

"Who is he?"

"Who is anybody?"

I was quiet and considered the name, as if there were clues in a name.

"How did you meet my mother?"

Dobbs smacked his parched lips. I wasn't about to offer to get him water. I hoped his cracked lips bled.

"I gave a sermon at a revival meeting. I was inspiring to so many. I spoke about the connection between a man and a woman and how a woman's sex was for male plucking."

I was feeling sick again. "What does any of that have to do with the Bible?"

"Everything." Dobbs set his dark, ugly eyes on me. "The Bible is about man's dominion over women. It is holy when a man takes ownership of a woman."

I chose to ignore the comment. "Mother saw you at a revival. She got religious?"

"Most people become religious at revivals. A good revival meeting can sway even the most closed of hearts."

"It wouldn't sway mine."

"You should go to one. With an open heart, of course."

"I think I'm done with you."

"Don't leave." Dobbs's voice had an elevated pitch.

"Go fuck yourself. You probably can't do that. Jerk off. I bet you want to. I bet your just burning with desire. Too bad you can't do anything about it. Dumb-ass. You do know that your interpretation of the Bible is only informed by your horniness." I stood and headed to the door.

"Petra, Petra." Dobbs's voice rang across the room. The old man with the James Patterson book finally lifted his head and peered in my direction. His eyes had been glued to the page the whole time, even when I nearly tilted the wheelchair. I walked back to Dobbs.

"What?"

"Are you saying you aren't burning with desire?"

"I hope you die, painfully."

I left the room and walked past the front desk quickly.

"Ma'am, ma'am." I turned and saw the angular nurse standing front of the desk. "I was told there was in incident with Mr. Dobbs."

I said nothing and attempted to look unconcerned.

"I'm going to have to make a report to the proper authorities. I thought I'd let you know."

"When?" I asked.

"What?"

"When did you find out about this incident? Just now? Or right after it happened?

"What difference does it make?" The nurse was walking towards me.

"If you found out earlier, why did you let me stay in there?"

The nurse stopped walking and fiddled with the keys clipped to her pants.

"You figure out the answer to that question before you make any report."

I hurried to my car, pulled out and sped to the highway. If the nursing home made a report, I was going to have to explain everything to William. I considered telling him that evening instead of waiting for the report to land on his desk. Of course, if I waited, I had a better chance of maintaining innocence. I didn't do anything. More plausible if you didn't think there was something to share. William would be all levels of angry.

When I got home I was a mess, so I poured a hefty amount of gin into a glass, squinted my eyes and drank it as quickly as possible. I poured another glass and noticed I was getting low on gin. I went to the den to sit and I realized what I was feeling. Sex. And I didn't want sex with William. I didn't want sex with any measure of love. My laptop was sitting on the table and I opened it. I pulled up Red Tube. They had videos to recommend and I clicked on the first one. It was German porn. An older woman, late thirties, with a younger man. It should have been erotic but it wasn't. It was sexual. Only sexual. That's what I wanted. I pulled up my dress and rubbed myself. Not frantically. Relentlessly. I came easily and rested. I knew this was not the end of it. I clicked on another video and fingered myself until I came again. This went on for nearly two hours. I wasn't masturbating the whole time. Most of the time was spent lazily watching the videos. It was only when my body recuperated that I made an effort to make myself come again. I closed the laptop when I craved another drink. I staggered into the kitchen and found the nearly empty bottle. I drank from the bottle that time. I sucked down every gorgeous drop and then stared at it and wondered how something became nothing. Pressure released from my chest and I began sobbing, releasing waves of sorrow into the universe of my home, and very near collapsing. I staggered once more, except this time onto the living room couch. I let my emotions peak and collapse until I felt as if they had been hung to dry in the unwelcoming air. Wasted on the couch, I whimpered like an injured animal who had come to terms with dying. I assumed William would eventually leave me. How could he not? I was a bad person. I told Dobbs I wasn't, but I didn't really believe it. William would be so much happier with another woman who actually took care of the house, hosted parties, and gave him children. Maybe I could find a replacement wife. The sooner the better. I didn't want him to suffer. I thought of the ad I would post to find him a new wife. I wrote and edited it in my head as I drifted off to sleep.

I was awakened by William stroking my hair. He was leaning over me on the couch.

"You've been asleep a while." He was smiling at me and then wiped saliva from the corner of my mouth.

"What time is it?"

"Almost six. Let me sit down, sleepy girl."

I moved my legs off the couch and he sat down and pulled me tightly into him.

"What made you so tired?"

Half of my mouth was pressed against his chest. His chest was hard and unyielding, and yet it gave more comfort than a woman's. I inhaled his scent, which was lacquered with something new. I sniffed and sniffed.

"What do you smell?" He sounded paranoid.

"Like...chemicals...formaldehyde..."

"Oh, I was at the lab today. If only you could solve crimes with your nose."

"The girl crucified? My sister?"

"That's basically the only major case we have going on at the moment."

"Why haven't you solved it?"

"Good question."

"Do you find it more than coincidental that my sister should end up murdered on the only highway turnoff that leads to the town where mother and I lived? And mother is likely alive somewhere out there."

"It's not coincidental, I'm sure. But I'm reluctant to know where any of it goes, as it would involve you at some point and I need you safe."

"You can't protect me from the outside world. Not completely. And you have a duty to the victim."

"I know. Of course, I also have a duty to you. I'd rather protect you at the expense of my job."

I started crying once again. Of course, the valves were never really shut off. My energy had just waned. The passion for sobbing was still there.

"Why are you crying?" William kept his hand on my head so that it was pressed against his chest.

"I don't think I'm good enough for you," I practically mumbled through a sheet of tears.

William didn't say anything but I felt him kiss the top of my head. My crying ebbed and I wiped my tears on his shirt.

"What happened today, Petra?" His voice was calm and inviting.

I inhaled and sniffled. "Nothing..."

"Petra. Can you please tell me?"

"I...I went to see Dobbs."

I was expecting him to push me away and pace the room. I was expecting anger and derision. William never met my expectations.

"That must have been hard for you." His voice was still as calm as a temperate summer lake.

"We talked about ice cream." I explained the bizarre conversation. I also shared what he told me about my mother. I left out the part where I nearly tipped him over in his wheelchair.

"I really wish we could have prosecuted him. The statute of limitations ran out with you and his son."

"He did tell me something. A name. Tyson Yeager. Have you ever heard the name?"

"I haven't, no. I'd have to run it through our database. It could be nothing, Petra."

"I wanted to talk to him. I wanted to find out what he offered her that was so wonderful. I want to know what was so wonderful that she had to trade me in for it."

"You're looking for answers that you probably shouldn't get. You mother was a horrible person. There doesn't have to be a reason for it. You just need to accept it."

"I can't just accept it without answers. I can't." I sat up and William's arm fell to my waist. "That woman ruined my life and I have to know why." I stood and smoothed my wrinkled dress. "I don't even know why she married dad. Their relationship seemed painful."

"Did you wonder why your father left?"

"All the time. My parents' desertion of me is partly why I am the way I am. And it's why I am certain you will abandon me, and that maybe the best thing is to prevent that by selecting someone for you." I was surprised I said it and that the idea was still so prominent in my mind. As I sat cuddled against him, I had been thinking that I would miss him terribly when he was with a new woman.

William stood. He looked more weary than calm. "You need to stop obsessing over the possibility of my abandoning you. I don't take marriage lightly, and I'm annoyed that you keep doubting my love for you. After all that we've been through and after knowing you, all the intimate details, you should recognize that my love for you is genuine."

He walked towards me and I, in an unfortunate reflex, backed away. "Why don't I know the intimate details about you?"

"Do you ask?"

"Yes, I do ask. You told me I could ask anything, but when I ask you shut down or give vague answers. It feels lopsided. You have all this information about me and I have none about you."

"You have some information. You're being dramatic. And it makes me uncomfortable talking about myself. I'm not hiding anything. My history is just not as complicated as yours."

"Tell me about your parents."

"Now?" He was exasperated.

"See? You don't want to share." I started walking away.

"Alright. I'll talk about them. My mother…"

"You don't have to talk about them."

"I thought you wanted to know." Exasperation was now a mainstay of his tone.

"I don't want to know about your boring family right now."

"Damn it." He shook his head.

"I'm changing my clothes." I pulled my dress off before I was in the bedroom. It didn't seem likely I would ever wear the dress again as it had the taint of Dobbs. William came up behind me and kissed the scar on my shoulder. I turned around and kissed him, expecting a new smell or taste, but it was the William I had grown accustomed to. My libido was truly spent, but the way William was kissing me let me know it wasn't sex he was chasing. It was love. I let him lead me to our bed and allowed myself to be loved.

Chapter 8

I had no story I was comfortable telling. Not in print. The *White Mountain Times* approved a story on the victim. I didn't know she was my sister. I didn't know my DNA was intertwined with the case. I needed a new story. I needed to write something. Something more than Brechtian visions.

I called Charlene at the newspaper. "Charlene? Petra. Checking in."

"Do you have the story on that poor girl?"

"Things were getting sticky between my husband and me."

Charlene was silent, and I couldn't tell if she was angry or distracted. "You should have told me earlier. I'll get it reassigned. Why else are you calling?"

"I still want to do a story. I heard about these weird revival meetings and thought I might go to one. Do you know where they are? I didn't see anything on Google."

"You're not going to find them on Yelp. Most of the meetings take place at a field outside Snowflake. On Sundays, of course. You won't make this week's deadline. Do you have anything you can give me for this week?"

I didn't have anything. "A new antique store opened in Pinetop. I could interview the owner and get some pictures."

"That's fine. Our readers like that stuff. Hey, can you leave out any literary or philosophical stuff? Our readers don't like that." Telling me not to do that was like telling me to write backwards.

"Will do." I clicked off the phone. I pulled up the website for Lazy Jane's antique store on my laptop and called the number. The owner picked up and I spoke with her and was able to do a decent interview over the phone. For the next hour I worked on the article and checked my email. I had a decent draft, so all I needed to finish was for the owner to email me photos. I sat back and felt mildly productive for the day and I nearly forgot all the other consuming things in my life.

Around 2PM, I got a call from a local number. The number looked familiar but I couldn't place it. Against my better judgment, I picked it up.

"Petra?" The voice was professional but airy. The voice was familiar...Marge. Why was she calling?

"Yeah." As a former interrogator and military police, I knew to hold back with law enforcement or anyone else in authority.

"How are you? Marge here. I got a call from a nursing home in Show Low." Wonderful. The nurse bitch called the authorities like she promised. I had my defense. I was quiet. I would make Marge work for this questioning. "A witness said you attempted to tip a man over in his wheelchair."

"Really?" I stood up and poured a glass of gin and tonic.

"Yes." Marge was making an effort to sound pleasant. I could tell. She didn't even start off with small talk.

"Was anybody hurt?" I attempted to sound concerned.

"No..." Marge was losing some power in her questioning. Really, Marge? All I did was play the quiet and vague card.

"What's the problem?"

"You almost caused injury…"

"I did? Me? Care to tell me who we're talking about?"

"Last name Dobbs…"

"Oh, him. That's not what happened."

"What happened?"

"He wanted me to adjust his sheet he was wrapped in and I did a poor job because I caused the wheelchair to tip, slightly, but I fixed the problem. That's it."

"Oh." You're not supposed to say that, Marge.

"Has Dobbs explained the situation?"

"He isn't talking. He refuses."

"He's a character, that one. Is there anything else?"

"I may need to make a referral to Adult Protective Services. Just letting you know."

"Okay, Marge. You do what you need to do. However, in working for child protective services I can confidently state that nothing will come of his. The nursing home should have addressed the matter when it was observed instead of triggering a line of institutional involvement."

"I still need to assess this matter in light of other interviews." Marge was trying to sound authoritative.

"Okay. Hey...does the Sheriff know?"

"Of course, he assigned this matter to me. If I need any more information, I will call." Marge hung up the phone without another word. It was a weird phone call from someone who had invited you into their home and fed you prime rib. I set Marge aside. William was the issue. He didn't even call me to give me the heads up. And why assign the matter to Marge rather than the five other deputies? I did what I rarely did. I called him. He didn't pick up until the fourth ring.

"I'm going to have to call you back. In the middle of something. Is everything all right?" William's voice had an icy calm, except there was an edge. Something was cracking the calm.

"Bye."

I threw the phone down on the dining room table where I had set up my notebooks and laptop. I went to the couch where my books were splayed. I picked up *Death in Venice* by Thomas Mann. Around four, I checked my email and saw the pictures from the antique store. I read the article again, made some changes, and then sent it off along with the photos. Sunday I would seek God in Snowflake. My phone rang, I saw it was William, and I ignored it. I was halfway done with *Death in Venice.* I'd read it before. Several times. I never ceased to be moved by it. I kept reading. The sun faded, I turned on lights, and poured another drink. Back to the couch. It wasn't until almost six that William came home. He looked neither worn out nor agitated. That was William. He never looked emotional unless he wanted you to see his emotions.

"How was your day?" he asked.

"Splendid." It actually wasn't a bad day. It just got thrashed a bit by Marge.

William's eyeballs were latched onto my eyeballs. It could have been romantic if not for resentment by each of us.

"Go ahead. Speak your mind, Petra."

"Whatever do you mean, husband?" I gave him the courtesy of closing the book.

"What did you do, wife?" William leaned forward. His evening stubble looked shaded and I realized a few gray hairs had sprouted with the whiskers. That was new. Was I doing that to him?

"I didn't do anything."

"Good, don't tell me anything. Please. It'll put me in an odd situation." He sat back and extended his legs. His eyes were starting to look tired.

"Nothing happened. Why didn't you give me the heads up?"

"I couldn't do that. No, I could do it except it wouldn't have been ethical." William reached into this pocket and pulled out his cell phone. It was lit up with text messages.

"Why did you assign Marge?"

"She's one of the least effective deputies in the department." William was tapping text messages.

"Are you mad at me?"

William glanced up. "No, Petra. I'm not. It was just an awkward situation. Hopefully, your police and interrogation skills kicked in."

"Marge isn't very good at interviewing."

"I know. I truly know. Is there dinner?" The question was full of hope.

"Have to make it."

"What's stopping you?"

"Gin and Mann." I finished off my drink for emphasis.

"Sounds like a poem."

"Don't worry, husband. I will make dinner." I reluctantly went to the kitchen with a dread of cooking. There was, thankfully, food from my last market trip and I was able to pull something together in twenty minutes. I pushed aside my computer and made room on the dining table. William wandered in and I served him and we both ate. We were lost in our own thoughts, his likely were on work and mine were on Venice, desire and death. After dinner, I kept reading and then went to bed early. The medication was kicking in and was helping me sleep. William joined me not long after.

"What is so interesting in your book?" I could feel William's breath on my cheek.

"Desire. It never ends." I felt a centimeter of numbness. The meds were spilling over my brain. Huge cascades of chemical quenching. Soon I would stop masturbating. Soon I would stop wanting sex. I didn't consider that a good thing. Desire was terrible and it was undeniably beautiful.

"And you have desire?" He sounded innocent.

"Constant." Until the meds win the war.

"What do you desire?" It was a trap question. My brain was on high alert.

“You. Mostly.”

“You desire me?” He actually sounded surprised. I was surprised he let “mostly” go by.

“You know I do. I think about you constantly. Not just sex. I imagine a finger on one inch of your skin so I can feel the heat, texture, and that consuming feeling that gives me a little summer in my soul. And then I think of your smile. The frown lines you tend to get when you look at me…” There was so much and I had never vocalized any of them.

“You never told me that. Why not?”

“You already think I’m crazy.”

“I don’t. You keep saying that, but I don’t. I think…” His voice trailed off and he sounded melancholy.

“What?” I turned my head towards him.

His eyes were closed as he spoke. “There’s this vast ocean of our soul we’re sailing on, and most things in our life are only on the surface of the water or just below and then there’s you, who came from the deep, and wrapped your arms around me. You pulled me into the water, but you won’t let us go too deep. You keep us near the surface – acceptable, usual, and pedestrian. You’re keeping us from being completely over our heads. I want to be over my head, Petra. I want to be so far below with you that I hope I never find my way back up…I figured you didn’t love me enough…I…”

He turned onto his back and wiped the corner of his left eye. I couldn’t tell if he was crying. He opened his eyes and stared at the ceiling. I couldn’t detect anything in the dark. I didn't know what to say. I was preventing the deepening of a mutual obsession that was laden with love. In December, I was certain we were on the path to the kind of relationship I had fantasized about since my teen years. But I pulled away in a myriad of ways, and in our lovemaking I never allowed myself to be at the point of complete abandonment. I can't blame my history and mental illness. There was another reason. What if living in the deep with William was not enough? What if it failed to meet my fantasy expectations? What else would there be? I would have a desire that could never be met. It would last until death.

I raised myself up. "Listen to me, it has nothing to do with my love or desire for you. It's fear. My fear."

"How can we address it? I don't want to feel like our marriage is a shadow of some more vibrant form out there."

I didn't know what to say.

"It's a struggle to have you be vulnerable with me."

Now I was angry. "Don't put this all on me. Do not. I still don't know your life. You failed to introduce me to your mother and father. All the meetings with your friends and family were awkward. I never know what really goes through your mind. You keep your emotions in check with me. I rarely know if you even desire me. How can we address your obvious lack of vulnerability?"

He was silent, and then sat up on his elbows. "I've been to blame. I think I was punishing you. After your injury, you were so open to me. It was beautiful. You were vulnerable and you were the most beautiful I had ever seen you."

"I was wounded."

"Wounded and bleeding, and you allowed your soul to bleed. You wrote the other day. Did you bleed on the page?"

"No."

"If you allow yourself to bleed, you could write."

"I could fix us?"

"I would serve you my soul at every mealtime."

I lied down and curled up. "Our marriage is barely two weeks old and I've managed to destroy it."

"What are you saying? Our marriage is fine. I love you. I could live for the rest of my life like this and die happily. I think both of us want more, though. We both have an idea of a relationship in our heads. Maybe it's unrealistic. Maybe it doesn't exist. I think we know otherwise."

"What do you think of? When you think of that relationship?"

He wrapped his arm around me. "I think, don't laugh, of washing your hair and watching the soap drip and swirl at your feet and your clenched eyes afraid of being stung. When your hair is soap free, you kiss me and smile and then I towel you off."

"That's it?"

"There are other thoughts. I like that one."

"You could do that now."

"No. It's the look on your face. Trusting, happy, unashamed. You have the look of a child."

My heart sank. "I don't think I looked like that when I was a child."

"You can mend. There's time. I'm not going anywhere."

I had my doubts of mending – mending the child from long ago. I thought about how to do that as I felt William's arm grow heavy. He was falling asleep and already I could hear his exhausted, ragged breathing.

In the morning, I attempted breakfast but scorched the eggs. William ate them without comment, kissed me good bye, and then left for work. I busied myself with reading, failed writing, and then began researching vulnerability. It had something to do with not being afraid of your feelings and emotions and feeling yourself worthy of positive emotions. It was also not about anger and hatred but love. I had my doubts about the whole concept. I supposed that was another symptom of my invulnerability. I was on some blog, can't remember which one, and it stated that it is only when there are no walls around us that we are safe. That was a downright revolutionary idea. Imagine if governments the world over took that one to heart.

I spent the rest of the week in the same manner. Saturday was more eventful, as William was home for part of the day until he got called out on what sounded like a drug matter. On Sunday I awoke to an empty bed. I found William in his office sorting through mail. There was a stack for me I had been ignoring and would continue to ignore. There were still no buyers for my house, and my bank account was dwindling.

William would easily loan me money, or even pay my bills, but I felt uncomfortable asking him. Was that invulnerability?

"I'm going to Snowflake."

William was reading the electric bill. He stared at me. "Why?"

"I'm looking for a revival meeting. Dobbs mentioned he and mother, Marnie, met at one. Apparently, they happen in Snowflake."

"I'm going with you."

"Are you sure?"

"Yes. I'm off today."

We left an hour later. It would take an hour and a half to get there if there was no traffic and minimal trucks. I was dressed in black. I might have looked dressy if not for the fact I was wearing a tight t-shirt. William spent the drive talking about his childhood friends and I smiled because he shared the stories. It was interesting how we were both making an effort to share and, in my case, be less sarcastic and repulsed by domesticity.

"Do you know where we're going?"

"Some field. I don't know where."

William kept his eyes on the road. "I think I know where. I had to come out here several months ago. It was at a revival meeting. Two men got into a knockdown, drag-out fight over a woman. I think it's about three miles up." He drove slower than usual as he was trying to remember the location of the tents. We drove for several miles, and then William pointed at tents in the distance. People had parked on the unpaved field.

William drove up and parked several yards from the last car. There were three tents; two were white and one was red. There was a sign on one of the white tents which rippled in the breeze. The lettering was in black and was in a highly readable font. God's Daughter and Unending Desire. The sign made me both trepid and interested. Unending desire? Had they read my thoughts? There were people sitting on folding chairs in every tent. There was also a stage and podium in each tent. The red tent was larger than the other two and the people in the tent seemed hyper. They were shouting, throwing their arms up, muttering things. I went to the tent that had the sign. A middle-aged man with a pointy chin was making statements and hitting the Bible at the same time. He was talking about the meaning of sacrifice and why God sacrificed Jesus. William pulled me towards him.

"What are you hoping to find here?" he whispered.

I wasn't sure.

"We won't be long. I promise."

Children were playing in the field, and several were clustered around a long table selling water and food. The adults were mostly in the tents, but I could see several in the field and hanging around near the outhouses. William and I were not quite inside the tents. We were listening skeptically along the edges. There was an uncoordinated lull, and then I heard a single female voice, loud and articulate. It sounded oddly familiar. I couldn't place it. I might have heard it on the radio or TV. I walked toward it. It was coming from the red tent. There were rows and rows of chairs stuffed with people.

"Desire is not an abomination. Desire is the reason for existence. Desire keeps life interesting. It is when desire leaves that you must be concerned. When desires dies, so do you. The desire between a man and a woman, that desire, is holy. There need not be love. All you need is desire. Don't expect that desire to make you whole. We can never be whole. There is a part of our soul, like a dried lake across a plain, which can never be filled. Don't look to your husband or wife to fill it. Accept its existence. When you die it will be no more."

The woman was dressed in an expensive white suit and on her feet were nude-colored designer shoes. Her long red hair stretched down to her waist, and it undulated in the early spring wind. I knew if I gazed at her face I would recognize the freckles. What shape would I see now? A heart? A cross? The form of a deserter? My mother. I couldn't call her that. She hadn't been my mother for many years. She was barely my mother when I lived with her. Marnie. Marnie Blue. She probably wasn't a Blue anymore. She probably wasn't Marnie anymore. The aging vision before me was polished, well-dressed, well-spoken and nearly unrecognizable from the woman I knew if not for her voice, gait, and knitting of the brow. Freckles would be another revealing element, except I couldn't see them from where I was standing.

I pulled on William's pant loop. "That's my mother." I seemed as placid as a sunflower in a cow pasture. Emotions were frothing and I decided to allow them to. It is when I try to control my emotions that they become uncontrollable.

William laughed. "You're kidding?"

I shook my head. "Why would I kid about that?"

"Jesus Christ." His jaw dropped slightly.

"Those are appropriate words for here."

The sermon went on and on regarding the same themes. The union between a man and a woman, the holiness of desire, the emptiness inside us we would never fill. It was making me horny and sad at the same time, and I was sure it was having the same impact on the audience. I noticed there were only babies and no older children. They must have been banished by their parents to the field. The sermon ended with The Lord's Prayer, an oddly traditional choice for an atypical sermon. I wasn't sure whether to leave or stay. I wanted to do both, and if I did either I would be unhappy. Marnie exited the stage and then went down the aisle shaking hands, answering questions, waving, fussing over babies. She was like a movie star dealing with fans at an awards show or a politician seeking re-election. I stood with William at the very end of the main aisle and waited. When she was a few handshakes away she eyed me and smiled. I didn't see recognition. I moved forward and after another handshake we were face to face at an even eye level. I saw her freckles clearly. I started connecting them into shapes.

"So good of you to come to the sermon." She shook my hand. Her hand was smooth, soft and dry. No drop of perspiration.

"Do you know who I am?" I opened my eyes wider.

She kept smiling with her perfectly capped teeth. But then her eyes became impenetrable and I saw her back stiffen. "No. Who are you?"

"You haven't seen me for a while. You put me in a car, drove me to Dobbs, and then took off to make riches."

"Petra." It wasn't a sigh. It was closer to an insult.

"Mother."

We stared at each other for several moments. There were no gushing feelings. She relented, softened and went back to smiling. The hard fucking eyes were still there. William came up and put his hand on my back.

"Who is this?" She asked in a singsong voice.

"My husband," I said.

She laughed lightly. "Well, aren't you handsome? I bet she keeps a tight rope on you."

"It's nice to meet you. I'm...what is your name?"

"Vanessa Tweed."

I laughed and they looked at me. "Tweed? That's the name you chose?" I wasn't sure why it was so funny.

"I married again. Dear man. He died in a fire."

I remembered William had told me her last known address was an apartment building. I wondered if she started the fire to rid herself of her husband. She took me to a pedophile to get rid of me. She was capable of anything.

"I'm sorry to hear that," William said.

"Why did you do it, Vanessa?" I spoke her name with extreme acid.

"What?" She looked innocent.

"Get rid of me."

Vanessa kept smiling. "I can't discuss anything here. Walk with me. You too, handsome." She walked to a van that was open in the back. A man in black was standing there, looking emotionless. Vanessa removed her high heels and encased her feet in slip-on sneakers. She also took off the expensive white jacket and put on an equally expensive cashmere button down sweater. She walked us out past the parking area.

"You look well, Petra. You don't look quite how I thought you would turn out. With your father's dark looks from his Yaqui heritage I was expecting you to look more exotic. I see your freckles never faded and your eyes seem more grassy green now than as a child. You look like the girl next door if you lived in Staten Island. You're pretty, though you miss the mark on ravishing somehow. You were such a dark baby. Nobody doubted you were Yaqui then. I was certain my fair Irish blood would desert you. But here you are with those freckles and those eyes."

"You look different, Vanessa. Your designer clothes, the more developed makeup, the hair. It looks redder now. You must be dyeing it. Let's not stop at appearances. You sound different. Gone is the filthy, angry mouth."

"We all change with time. Except for some things. I bet you're still a bookworm, aren't you? Tendency to be morose? Is that true?" She looked at William.

"She likes to read." He didn't sound happy about having to respond to her.

"She always did. Before she could even read she clung to books."

"You never answered the question. Why did you leave?" My emotions were going in an out like the tide.

"I didn't like my life. I didn't like where I was living. I needed an escape. Dobbs gave me one."

"At a price," I reminded her. "The price of a daughter."

She ran her hands through her lengthy hair. "Petra, let's be honest. We didn't like one another. You know it's true."

"I was a child." I threw that one like a fastball.

"Who didn't like me. I'm not even sure what you liked other than books. You had no friends, sports, social interests."

"You gave me to a pedophile." My soul was quaking.

"Dobbs? Was he?"

"You know he was." I screamed and an arrow of low flying black birds rustled. "He was a sexual maniac. And you know this because you met him at a sermon, like this revival, where he apparently said the same crap you do. You knew what you were getting me into. That day he first came to the house and you prayed with him, that didn't seem odd to you? Ever so slightly, mother?"

"How do you know this?"

"I remember things. Also, Dobbs is sitting in a nursing home in Show Low. He provided some information. He told me about these revivals. I wouldn't have come here if he hadn't."

Vanessa (strange calling her that) smoothed her hands over skirt. "What happened with Dobbs?"

"I'm not discussing that with you. I will say he committed grievous crimes. Not only against me but other children."

She swallowed and I saw sinews on her neck tighten and release. "I'm sorry about that. I didn't know."

"You abandoned me. Has the statute of limitations run?" I turned to William whose face was pale and hard.

"Petra…"

"It has, hasn't it?"

Vanessa looked at William and then me. "How would he know?"

"He's the Sheriff. He should know."

Vanessa's eyes went wild and fearful. She backed up a step and then steadied herself. She gave a tight smile.

"Petra, you obviously have things to say to me and I want you to say them. Maybe it would be better if it was just you and me present when you did."

I started to protest but William spoke. "Why don't you two walk further out in the field? I'll stay here and watch."

I didn't think I wanted to be alone with her. "But…"

"Yes, Petra. Let's just take a small walk."

I followed her lanky legs out onto the hard soil. There were patches of mud that I circumvented, but mostly the soil was still hard from winter. As I watched her walk a few paces ahead of me, I realized that I never really loved her as a mother. I was a child and I needed her. That was not love. I thought it was. Children are supposed to love their parents. If you don't love them they might not feed you. Loving a parent is not without a degree of unstated coercion. As I thought about my lack of love for her, I realized I also did not love my father as he was too frequently absent, silent, and made no effort to actually connect with me. Both parents were quick to hit, repeatedly, and did not stop, even when I screamed or cried. It's a sad moment when you realize you didn't love your parents. I was despondent as I walked with Vanessa further out into the field. I needed to be free of her. She had loomed so large in my mind for so long, and as I stared at her freckled calves, I realized I could leave her be. My questions had been answered. I never had hopes of a teary reunion and my arms encircling her lively neck. I needed, for some mysterious and possibly primitive reason, to see her flesh, to hear her voice, to watch her facial expressions, as doing so would solidify my past memories and confirm that her life went on after she abandoned me. When I was with Dobbs and in that dim house, I obsessed over her and wondered if she were even alive.

"I truly had no idea about Dobbs." She had stopped and looked back at the tents and the empty makeshift parking lot. William could be seen walking back and forth like a cornered animal.

"You did. I wish you would stop saying you didn't."

"I'm sorry."

"We don't have to continue this conversation. I have what I need. I learned what I needed to learn."

Vanessa looked curious. "What is that?"

"That I never loved you and you never earned the title, mom." As I said that, I remembered something significant. "There was a girl crucified at the Greer exit. Long red hair. Probably ten years younger than me. Turns out we share DNA. Did you know your daughter was murdered a few days ago?"

Vanessa said nothing and eyed me with hostility, suspicion, and something I couldn't identify, or at least I hadn't seen in a while. I think I recalled seeing it in the prisoners, the ones we arrested for terrorism. It was in their eyes. Why was it in Vanessa's eyes? With no prior clue, she began crying. No tears slid down her face. Not at first. I didn't say anything. Fake sobs.

"I hadn't seen her in over five years. What was she doing here? I wonder if she was coming to find me."

"You better let William know. They're going to have to release the body to someone. You're her mother." Vanessa quivered and shivered in the March sun. I had one last question. "Were we alike at all?"

Vanessa wiped tears from her eyes. "Reading. You both loved reading."

I thought about that. It would have been nice to have a sister to talk about things with. "What was her favorite book?"

Vanessa kept wiping flowing tears. "She had so many. The book I saw her with the most was *The Threepenny Opera*. Do you know it?"

Did I know it? I just wrote my own opera. "Yeah. It's important to me too." I walked away from Vanessa. She called out to me but I ignored her. William was leaning on his car attempting to look casual, though I knew he was tense and concerned. I rushed up to him and fell into his arms.

"Everything will be fine," he said in between kissing my head.

"I'm done with her." I stretched and kissed William on the mouth. "But you should get her info. She claims she hadn't seen my sister for over five years. Didn't really deny knowledge of the crucifixion, though."

"She has to come down to the station. I knew that when you recognized her. I thought I would let you two mend, or try to."

"Do you have to take her to the station now?"

William shook his head. "I called two of the deputies on duty today. They should be here in thirty minutes. Let me go talk to her."

William walked out onto the field and Vanessa looked welcoming as he approached. They chatted, at least it seemed like chatting, as Vanessa smiled and edged closer to him, and then they walked together toward the red tent. I walked around our car and came upon Vanessa's car. The back was closed and a muscular man with an attractive, hard set face sat in the driver's seat with a Bluetooth in his ear. I didn't think he was her boyfriend. He looked too official. He looked paid for. As I was passing the car, the man got out and walked toward me. He was good-looking, but there was a smugness to his look, an overabundance of self-confidence, which made him less attractive. He was over six feet tall and I had a wild sensation of being unsafe around him. He smiled at me, ear to ear, and revealed exact, medium sized white teeth. His eyes were grassy green like mine.

"Did you enjoy talking to Vanessa?" he asked.

"Not really."

His smile did not waver. He adjusted his belt by moving it incrementally to the left. "Most people enjoy talking to her."

"Who are you?" I asked.

"Who are you?"

I was no longer in the mood for secrets. "I'm her daughter. The one she abandoned years ago. My name is Petra. Your turn?"

His eyes became turbulent and his body seemed to tighten slightly. "My name's Matthew. I'm a friend of Vanessa's."

I nodded at him and then walked off. I saw a Sheriff's car several yards ahead, pulled up next to the red tent. William was standing and Vanessa was sitting with a bottle of water. There were two deputies standing next to William. Vanessa wouldn't even glance at me.

"What's going on, Vanessa?" Matthew was walking towards the group. I was standing apart from everybody.

"Oh, Matthew, Kristin is dead. They found her a few days ago in some kind of macabre scene. I need to go to the station and tell them all I know and tell them my whereabouts. They'll take me. Can you meet me at the station? I want to do what I can to help with the investigation."

"Vanessa, don't worry. I will meet you over there."

William was assessing Matthew and trying to determine the connection between him and Vanessa. It was the same thing I had done.

"Did you know Kristin?" William asked in an even, nice tone.

Matthew shook his head. "Sorry to say, I did not. I heard she was a lovely girl, though."

"Vanessa, we should get you to the station. I'm sure you want to salvage what you can from your Sunday."

The deputies saw Vanessa to the squad car and spoke with William briefly. Matthew watched and then headed to his car without a glance at me. William walked over and took me by the elbow. He guided me towards his car.

"I'll take you home and then go over to the station. I want Vanessa to sit awhile."

We rode in silence for the first few miles.

"What was it like?" he asked.

"It was like turning on the stovetop and expecting flame and only getting cold blankness."

"You handled yourself well. I love you." He rubbed his hand up and down my thigh.

"She seemed to like you."

"It's my magnetic good looks." He laughed lightly.

"Seriously."

"She was trying to irritate you. It had nothing to do with me. You didn't see that?"

I shook my head. "I was too focused on feeling ill."

"What do you think of her story regarding Kristin?"

"Lies. Your interview should be interesting."

"I'm going to be a while."

"Okay. I'll probably go to the store and get something for dinner. You'll be home eventually."

Around one in the afternoon, William dropped me off at home. He didn't say much, though looked beleaguered and irritated at the prospect of hours of work, and attempted to relieve his frustration by spending several minutes kissing me. I waved good-bye and entered the empty house and couldn't quite stomach having it all to myself. I didn't want to read, write, or watch TV. I got my keys and purse and took off down the highway. I meandered around the roads for over an hour. I could have gone to the grocery store in Eagar but that would be too quick of a trip. I decided to drive into Pinetop-Lakeside. I stopped at what used to be regular hangout, The Lion's Den. It was a bar with decent food, particularly their onion rings, and excellent bands often played there. I doubted there would be a band on a Sunday afternoon and I was right. The place was unusually empty. There were only two people sitting at the bar, and they were focused on their burgers. I ordered a gin and tonic and a basket of onion rings. I considered what William said about bleeding on the page when I wrote and tried to figure out how to do that.

The bartender set the drink in front of me. "Do you know how to bleed on the page?" The bartender looked to be in his twenties with a floppy chunk of hair falling around his forehead.

"I think it means feeling something and not flinching and then sharing. And not caring about the judgment if you share." He pushed the chunk of hair back.

"Do you have an example of an author?"

He shrugged. "Most good ones do. Some squeak by without bleeding. I like Bukowski. He bleeds. You have to know what pains you and then you have to self-inflict a wound."

"Do you write?" I was intrigued.

He shrugged again. "Mostly poetry. I've been trying essays. What about you?"

"I write occasionally. I'm considering doing it more seriously."

"Don't consider. Do it. Silence the inner critic." He twirled his bar rag with his hands.

"I need to be vulnerable first."

"No way. You think Hemingway was vulnerable? You're just using it as an excuse."

"I have to figure out what I'm going to write."

"If you can't choose a plot then choose your life. I gotta go check on some customers."

"Because we all have a right to contribute a verse," I said, softly quoting *Hustle & Flow.*

I ordered another drink and finished my food. I waved to the bartender and left. I drove to the Fry's and bought groceries, a lot of them. It was similar to when you go shopping famished. I wasn't hungry. What I wanted was to provide a home for William and me, and that usually involves food. I stopped at the florist section and considered flowers. Lilies seemed funereal, red roses seemed like a special occasion, and the carnations were boring. That left the mixed bouquets and there was a spring mix with dappled yellow sunflowers, vivid turquoise blue carnations, pearly mums, baby's breath, and waxy, evergreen-colored foliage. I had a vase except it was buried in the garage in my multitude of boxes. William had no vases, so I bought a clear glass one. It felt liberating buying something that would die in a few days. In the past, I had rarely bought flowers or plants. I may have changed. I now saw the benefit in something flowering dying. Mother had once flowered in me, and now I could cast her into the wind.

The journey home was quick, as there was limited traffic and nearly no trucks on the road. I unloaded the car, put away the groceries and then arranged the flowers in the vase. The stems were tall so I snipped them. As I was doing so, I heard a car pull up. I opened the door and saw William walking up looking bedraggled.

"How did it go?" I asked.

"She gave limited information and has, apparently, a solid alibi for the time of death for Kristin."

"What's her alibi?"

William came in the door and hugged me. "Matthew."

"I don't think that's solid."

"He has a plane ticket for Florida. They were in Florida together. And he could never be pressed on it in court as his attorney would just assert the spousal privilege." William saw the flowers and went up and touched a carnation.

"Spousal privilege?"

"They're married."

That was a surprise. He seemed like he was the help.

"How exactly does she make her money?" I was curious.

"Import and export. The product is carpets. I have people at work checking all this information. I asked Vanessa to remain in town for a few days. She insisted she needed to return to Louisiana in a day. If I have nothing to charge her with, I can't make her stay."

I twisted my finger into his belt loop. "I bought food. Lots of it." I demonstrated my domesticity and made dinner.

Lotte Lenya #3

I was sore and bruised after Matthew. Feeling my body again was actually a relief. I didn't mind the pain. I minded numbness. Matthew turned Macheath into a lambent icon. My love for Macheath, that I thought was receding, blossomed hugely in my chest after sex with Matthew. I longed for him in the quiet moments and those are the only moments that count. In those moments, you can be truly touched. I dressed quickly and wondered how I was going to live a life of unrequited love. During sex, I told myself I could place Macheath in a precious box somewhere where I could reach him if life got too lonely. The idea of setting Macheath aside help solidify a commitment to my path in life. After sex, those internal statements wavered like a flame. I said nothing to Matthew as I exited his home. The driver took me back to the swamp and I lied in bed and attempted to chart out my life. Mother was still doling out an allowance while I was in training. It was only when I began brokering deals that I would get money. A hefty commission is what she said. Commission. Move more girls, get more money. Send more girls to their doom and I could liberate myself. I really didn't have much of a future. I could eventually buy things and travel. Have affairs across the globe. But I would never know love, have a family, or an honest vulnerable connection with somebody. And there was also the love I had for Macheath. I wasn't suicidal. I just wished I was.

For the next four years, I lived an unreal life. I had frequent affairs with men I chose. I regularly chose not to have sex with those men who assumed I would. I learned to be wild and animal-like during sex. This is was not rooted in deep passion. Wildness distracted the men and me from the fact that I was not overly attracted to them, and prevented them from finding out that my sexual pleasure was minimal. Orgasms came easily with Macheath; now they fizzled out after only a glimmering moment or two. It was like a Fourth of July sparkler that never fully gets lit. I only managed an orgasm when I masturbated. Then I did not think of Macheath, as that would be too painful, but an ivory-colored void where no man existed.

Professionally, I had become fluent in Russian, Spanish and Czech. I had tutors in the US and when I traveled to Europe. On planes and during car drives I studied my workbooks. When I was able to read *The Cherry Orchard* without consulting a Russian language book, I felt successful.

The languages were the bright spots. The rest of my work was uncomfortable. One time I went to Prague and stayed at a grand hotel. Prague was beautiful, and I wanted to sense the city on its streets. I envisioned myself as a bloodhound seeking out the true Prague. However, not long after I arrived at the hotel I received a phone call.

"Mr. Kerensky is eager to meet you. We will send driver." The voice was male and heavily accented. It was neither an old nor young voice.

"I prefer to get there my own way."

"You have car?" The voice sounded curious.

"Taxi."

"No. It's safer with our driver. Outside thirty minutes."

He was curt, almost hostile and he elongated minutes into miiinuuutessss. I didn't care if it was dangerous. My death would be fine. It would be retribution for the victims. I dressed in Prada, decided to keep my hair down, went heavier on the make-up and went downstairs to wait for the car. It pulled up in the taxi area.

"Kristin Tweed?" The driver was muscled and grim.

"Yes." I got in and the car meandered through the city until we pulled up outside a building. I could read the sign. Computer School. The windows were boarded up and I was escorted to a side door. Inside there was light. Lamps emanated an ambient glow. I walked forward, and out of the shadows emerged a man, about 5'8' and trim, with a graceful carriage. He could have been a ballet dancer and might have been given Russia's passion for the ballet.

"Kristin." He said it without doubt. "You don't look how I imagined." I didn't ask what he imagined. "You're sophisticated."

I responded in Russia. "Youth does not bar sophistication, only knowledge gained from experience. I have done many of these deals in the past. I am struck how each one is unique, which makes it hard to draw from experience."

"Your Russian is excellent. Your pronunciation needs continued work. I commend you."

"Can we get down to business?"

"Will you share vodka with me?"

"Of course, I love vodka. One of the best vodkas I ever had was in Poland. I don't really know the name of it. It was velvet fire with frost at its core. It was almost a religious experience."

Mr. Kerensky smiled. "I'm sorry you did not have that experience with a Russian vodka. Please, have a seat." He motioned me to a modern cushioned chair upholstered in red leather. It was plush and I liked sitting in it in my Prada clothes.

"How many?" He asked as he uncorked an unlabeled, pink toned bottle and poured two fingers of vodka into each glass. He handed me one and he sipped from his as he sat back in a chair identical to mine.

"We can only transport twenty out of Greece. You will have to get them down to Greece."

He stared into his glass considering. "You can't do more."

"No." I drank. The vodka burned but did not delight.

"Funds?"

"Tomorrow via electronic transfer. Our shell to your shell."

He drank again. "Do you want to see the girls?"

I was going to say no. It was professionally prudent and would cement the relationship with Mr. Kerensky if I surveyed the goods. "Yes, of course."

"Drink your vodka."

I downed mine and Mr. Kerensky finished his in two swallows. "Follow me." I realized there were men, surrounding the room, hidden in the shadows with glinty guns. Mr. Kerensky led me down a wide hall. He motioned to a burly man in a t-shirt to open the double doors. Upon opening the door, there was a stench. Something fetid with notes of urine and fecal matter. It was a huge room, a flat lecture hall, and on the floor were mattresses, threadbare ones, and on the mattresses were girls. Most were teenagers. The rest were in their twenties. The girls were in various stages of being high. Those whose drugs were wearing off or who had just been injected were crying out in despair. The lucky ones were those knocked out and prostrate. A few eyes lit up when they saw me, thinking I might be their hope for escape. I didn't smile and placed a hand, gently, on Mr. Kerensky's arm. The light in those eyes died and yet another light was extinguished in my soul.

"Any virgins?" I asked.

"Triple the price and you can only have two. I usually sell the virgins at auction."

Many things in life were mysterious, but the male desire for virgin flesh was a grand mystery. It was counterintuitive. I assumed men would want a sexually mature and experienced women rather than a shy, bumbling virgin. My assumption was wrong because the virgins were lucrative business.

"Then we will take two. Thank you for showing me. Oh, and I don't want any meth users. You give me meth users and I stop doing business with you. I'll check between the toes of the girls you select."

Mr. Kerensky nodded then shrugged. "Why?"

"Do you need to ask? Teeth, Mr. Kerensky. It's hard to push a girl with bad teeth. I'm leaving. We can meet tomorrow to review the girls, finalize matters, and complete payment."

The driver took me back and I hailed a taxi and went to The Alcron restaurant where I dined primarily on seafood. It was dark when I headed back to the hotel and the city. I went to bed and the next morning completed my duties impersonally. One girl pleaded with me to help her. She was backhanded by one of Mr. Kerensky's bulging men. He would have done more if I hadn't stepped in and made a claim for undamaged goods.

I went back to New Orleans. I had my own loft downtown. I wasn't far from Matthew. My decor was cool and modern, and expensively framed surrealist prints hung on my walls. My home was fashionable and presentable and completely lacking in personality. In my third bedroom, which was kept locked, things changed. It was filled with bookcases stuffed with books. Almost all of it was literature. On the wall hung a huge photograph of Brecht in a quirky frame. The frame had hills and a coastline replete with palm trees. It was meant to be Los Angeles. There was even a Hollywood sign in one corner. I liked reading about Brecht's time in LA. He had been miserable, lonely, alienated, rejected, and yet he still kept writing screenplays. Over fifty of them. I kept trying to locate them. There was a Brecht museum in Germany that I intended to visit. They would know about those screenplays. On the other wall were photos of Lotte Lenya and Kurt Weill. I would sit in this room and allow myself to think of Macheath. Sometimes I would think of Schopenhauer. Macheath had taught me about him. If you accept that things will be imperfect, unfulfilling, and unrequited then you will achieve stability. Sometimes you will be happy. Almost accidentally. Sometimes you will get close to fulfillment. You will be happy. Don't expect any of it to last. Do you know, Macheath said, that Schopenhauer lived out his days alone? He didn't prefer it. That was how it happened. He didn't face the possibility of suicide each day. He kept working and thinking and sometimes he achieved happiness. Don't put the pressure of optimism on yourself, Macheath said. Allow yourself to be sad and miserable. When we allow that sometimes the greatest changes happen in our life. Sometimes we become heroes of our story.

Two days after my trip, I went to a local club where I had sold three girls. They had been blowing up my work phone about a girl. With my bodyguard, I showed up at the club in a tailored, pleated dress. I was attempting to look both innocent and professional. The owner, Dodge, was white with a dusty bald head. He had an earring in one ear and he typically wore turtlenecks despite the heat and humidity of New Orleans. All his employees were black and well dressed. None looked as strange as Dodge.

"What is the problem?" I asked.

Dodge clenched his hands. "You gave me a fucked up girl. Really fucked up."

"How so?"

Dodge's facial muscles tensed. "She's pregnant."

I stared at the ugly man and tried to hide my hostility. "That's what happens when you cum in a girl, Dodge."

Dodge slammed his arms down on the black, shiny bar. My bodyguard went into high alert. "She came to us pregnant. He said."

"Who's he?"

"My doctor. He checked her out and matched it when we got her. It doesn't add up. But...but...we're missing the big, the big, fucking point. I paid for a virgin."

This was a problem. "We'll take care of it and give you a replacement and refund. Can I see her?"

Dodge looked around at his men. "Why?"

"If we replace her we need to take her off your hands. She's our problem."

Dodge nodded. "Maurice, can you take her to the little bitch?"

Maurice was dressed in a gray suit and had skin the color of hot chocolate. He led us down a mirrored hall to a door. He unlocked it with a key he pulled from a clip on his belt. I noted what the key looked like. It was a storeroom, and there were boxes and piled up toilet paper in one corner. In another corner was a tiny girl with dark hair. She was in a tank top and skirt and she was crumpled on the floor. I approached and she moaned. I saw bruises, cuts and cigarette burns on her. I detected a small rounded belly. I was trying to remember her tormented face. I couldn't. There had been too many girls.

"What did you guys do to her?"

"You needn't concern yourself with that," said Maurice.

I looked at that hovering life on the floor and bled. A soul bleed. Life is only worth something if you make your soul bleed. Macheath would be so disappointed with me for what I was doing. He didn't provide me with the education I had so that I could do harm to others. What he offered was creativity and thought. Not violence and degradation. I offered my hand to the girl.

"I'm not going to hurt you. I'm going to help you." I kept my hand out and she slowly raised herself off the ground like Lazarus. There was an exit door on my right. It was likely locked and the key was on Maurice's belt. "Are you listening to me? Out that door is an alley. Run straight down..."

"What the fuck are you doing?" Maurice had his hand on his gun.

"I'm setting her free."

His face tightened. "Fuck you are, bitch." He unholstered his gun and my bodyguard, whom Maurice had forgot about, unholstered his and banged Maurice so hard on the back of his head that I heard a crunching sound. Maurice collapsed and his gun skidded.

I looked back at the girl who had watched the ordeal with wide eyes. "Listen to me. Go down the alley, then go right, run straight down for two blocks. On your left is Our Lady of Perpetual Sorrow. Go inside and ask for Father Dominguez. Tell him you are a victim of sex trafficking. They will help you there. Did you hear me?"

The girl nodded, still wide-eyed. I stooped down to Maurice, pulled his pants until I heard a jingle, reached under and unhooked the keys. The key that I memorized, faintly green edges, was in the middle. I tried it in the exit door and it turned. I knew it would. One room was unlikely to have two different keys. I checked for an alarm and saw a small sensor above the door.

"Are you ready? Remember to run." I opened the door expecting to hear continuous beeping, but there was only one small beep. I pushed the girl out.

"Run."

She ran, barefoot, down the alley strewn with used condoms and broken beer bottles. The girl did not look back. When she got to the end of the alley she turned right. I hoped there would soon be brightness in her life. My bodyguard had been watching me impassively the whole time. That's what he he's paid to do. I threw the keys by Maurice and I motioned for us to leave through the alley. We went the opposite way of the girl. We didn't run but we walked quickly. My driver was parked on the street, a hundred yards down from the club entrance. I rushed forward and got into the backseat. My bodyguard took his position in the front seat. We sped off. I knew my bodyguard would tell mother. She paid him, not I. It wouldn't take long for word to reach my mother. When I got home I changed into pants and poured myself orange juice. I needed something sweet and it was all I had. I started playing Van Morrison and sat in my chair and looked out at the New Orleans skyline. The sun was setting and the horizon looked iridescent. The Mississippi snaked its turbulent way below and sped onwards to the Gulf. I sat in the chair for several hours. Waiting. Crushing expectation. Waiting. I thought of Brecht in LA. Submitting screenplays and waiting for phone calls. Crushing expectation. I got up and went to my secret room and sat there thinking of the first time I was with Macheath. I was so innocent. Cloistered like a nun. And he enveloped me with tenderness. My body thrummed with his memory. Then the doorbell rang. This is it, I thought. I opened the door slowly and Matthew was standing there with a sweet smile. He was leaning on the door jamb.

"Hey. What're you up to?" There was a sultry look in his eyes. I wasn't fooled. There was some greater plan going on. I played along.

"Nothing. Lonely." I said it with a breathy sigh. Matthew encircled his hands on my waist and lifted me up. He swatted the door closed and then carried me into my bedroom. I assumed he was going to kill me. He began, in a way unnatural to him, to tenderly kiss me and slowly remove my clothes and then, after a great deal of cooing and stroking, he slowly entered me. It was odd. It was as if he actually performed this way in the past. I knew he had a specific woman in mind because I almost thought I heard her name in the midst of his long body kisses. Something with a V. He didn't make eye contact when he was inside me. He kept his eyes shut. He was gentle as he nudged deeper into me, but the way in which he pushed in made it seem like he was looking for a spot he'd found before with someone else. He gave up the search, his body slackened, and my legs closed together as he pulled his now tender penis out. We lied there for some time. I wondered what this had been about. And then I knew.

"You should pack. We have to go to Arizona. Greer. One of our houses has some girls and we need to process them. There are buyers in New Mexico."

"That's it?" I asked.

"Yeah, why?" He was staring at the ceiling.

"No reason." I grew quiet and wondered what would happen in Arizona. "Who is she?" I asked.

"Who?" He was still enraptured by the ceiling.

"The woman you're in love with."

I felt his eyes on me. "One day you'll know."

"What? You'll bring her to the company Christmas party?" I chuckled. "I'm sure I'll never meet her." Talking made me less nervous. "What made you fall in love with her?"

"Her smell, her intense eyes. A collection of things. Specific and not specific when part of the whole."

"I'm going to say that being in your twenties with big tits helps."

"You're making assumptions about me and women in general. It's not attractive."

I looked at him in confusion. "Are you a feminist? You can't be and do this job. You can't be if you work for my mother. She's a nut about women's sexuality."

He got out of bed and began dressing. "She advocates women being sexual and suffering no consequences for it. Sex workers and women who are promiscuous should suffer no criticism for their actions.

"She also believes men and women can't ever be connected. Not truly. She's wrong. I've been connected and it was the most beautiful part of my life. Mother's bitter and disillusioned because she has never known any connection."

Matthew's face looked a tad stormy. "Your mother has had a rough life. She was sexually abused by her father when she was a child. Of course, she's going to have issues connecting with a man. Abuse shapes your entire worldview. It becomes your philosophy and fools you into thinking you have reasoned with your views, but those views are a direct result of your abuse. You need to be kinder to her."

I listened to his brief tirade with curiosity and an increasing level of disgust. Was he in love with my fifty-six year old mother? And I've been having sex with a man who has had sex with my mother? My vagina felt dirty and there was no scrub brush I could stick up there to clean it. Eeewww. And he was in love. This wasn't for business reasons. He actually loved her. The sex abuse of my mother I didn't care about. It was obvious she had some past trauma. Why else would she be willing go into sex trafficking and then preach her poison on the side? No. Her abuse was not startling. Someone loving her was startling. How evil could a villain be if someone loved your very fiber, the fiber winding around the soul, and licked your childhood wounds?

"You need to get dressed and packed. There's a car downstairs. Our plane leaves in two hours."

It took me half an hour to pack. We got to the terminal as they were boarding. We were silent on the trip and I discouraged conversation by keeping my earbuds in. By the time we got to Greer it was nearing 3AM. Matthew drove us to the house and I stared at the surrounding blackness broken only by an occasional light. The house was a rambling, expensive chalet that had been refurbished by mother years ago. It was sitting on two acres of land studded with pine trees. The girls were usually kept in the back room on the lower level. I went into the house and reset the alarm as Matthew brought in our bags. There was a sound on the stairs and I froze. Out of the barely lit grayness emerged mother. She descended the stairs, one at a time. She was dressed casually and her hair was free flowing.

"Mom?"

"Matthew and I are in Florida."

I was confused. "What?"

"It's easy enough. Fake IDs, two stand-in people. When you know the people we know it's easy." She was at the bottom stair and looked curiously youthful. Her face was free of make-up and, from a distance, you couldn't see the webbing of crinkly wrinkles marring her fair, fair skin. I glanced at Matthew who seemed strangely relaxed. Love was near.

"Why didn't you just go to Florida?" Panic was surging.

"I had business to do here. Plus, I just love the mountain air and the scent of pine trees. I grew up in the White Mountains, do you know that?"

"Yes." She told me the first time we came here. I heard a rustling. Three of mother's men, brawny and weaponized, appeared from the dark of the living room.

"You should get some sleep. You've had a long day."

I retrieved my bag and went upstairs to my room. I couldn't sleep. I laid in bed, willing myself to come to terms with death. When you think clearly about death, about leaving everything behind, it seems less awful and more inevitable. The only thing that can tank clear thinking about death is regrets. Regrets can cause sobbing. I forced mine aside. Everyone should be allowed some respite before the end of all their days. Around five in the morning, as the darkness was giving way to encroaching grayness and the tops of the pine trees began to look distinct, I heard moaning. Successive waves of it drifting through my right wall. Mother's bedroom was next to mine. The voice was male, whimpering, tormentedly blissful. It was Matthew. Instead of recoiling and feeling disgust over my mother's sex life, I felt terribly sad because I once yearned and desired like that. Long ago. I never experienced it since Macheath, and then a regret blossomed and it was that I wished I had experienced eroticism more. Regret that I should have hunted down some man that, together, we could have carved a boat of feelings and sailed off in it like intrepid explorers. I'm unashamedly romantic. Knowing yourself before you die is a good thing.

I fell asleep. When the sun was soaking the room in golden drops, two of the armed men came in. One held me down and the other primed a syringe and injected me. It was likely heroin. That's what we gave the girls. All went black. Then I was awakened by voices. I was prostrate and I could feel the tickle of grass. My nose was very near the grass and the smell of it irritated my nose. I thought the rich plant sap would make me sneeze. It would be nice to sneeze. It would be something to do since the rest of my body seemed frozen. I tried flexing my big toe. It would not move. Of course, my brain was hardly in a position for giving orders. I saw two of the men looking down at me. They stooped and grabbed hold of my legs and arms and lifted me. I saw a hunk of wood. They laid me on the wood. Then they took off my clothes and left me lying naked on the wood. I couldn't fathom what was happening. Mother and Matthew came into view.

"God had a daughter. He had two daughters. He sacrificed them for our sins. Do not have pity for them. They are sinners. Their greatest sin is their lack of dedication to him. You have hurt me, Kristin. You betrayed me and what I've built. You've left me no choice. You must suffer, greatly. Do you have anything to say?"

My slow mind thought. I considered my last words but curiosity got the better of me. "You've two daughters?"

Mother walked away and Matthew wielded a hammer. "This is going to hurt," he said. He stretched my arm. "Do you want it in your wrist or hand?" I couldn't answer a question like that. "Fine, wrist." An incredible pain shot through my arm and I vomited. The men tipped me over to let the vomit trickle out.

"I want you to know that all those times I had to have sex with, you were terrible. I could barely stand it. I shouldn't say that to a woman dying. I think you should know the truth in your death." He went to the other side of me and extended my arm and hammered again. This time there was no vomit, but the pain was unbearable and I cried though poorly since my body was still paralyzed by the heroin. Matthew gazed at me. "I'm sorry. I know this hurts. I'll ask Vanessa if I can give you more drugs." He disappeared and then I willed it over. The whole wreck of life. My sobbing became even deeper. Matthew came back and spoke to one of the men and he withdrew a syringe from his pocket. He uncapped it, tapped it, and then stuck it in my stomach. It didn't take long for the drug to work and I passed out. I remembered nothing more. I didn't have a profound thought. My last thought was that life was enormously frustrating and tormenting. It was a wreck and I wanted off the spinning mad ride. At some point, in being passed out my heart stopped and it was over. Brecht's Macheath was rescued. Most of never are.

Chapter 9

It was morning, Monday, but very early, and William was still in bed looking decidedly reluctant to get out of it. It probably didn't help that I had my breasts smashed against him.

"Mom used to have this way of smothering me. If I was sick she would rush into my room, pull the covers around me, jam a thermometer in my throat, and talk about what a sweet kid I was and how she loved me so much."

"Sounds horrible," I said jokingly.

"It was. It was such a burden. I felt obligated to be the sweet, perfect kid so she could have the love she wanted and required. If I messed up once, even if it was minor, she acted like I was intentionally condemning her to a life of loveless loneliness. I think she loves me more than my dad. I think. I'm not sure. I'm telling you because that is why I didn't introduce you to my parents. It had nothing to do with you. It was me. I couldn't deal with the recriminations, the smothering and then the withholding, and her suffering. I should've dealt with it, for you. I'm sorry."

I kissed his chest. "It's fine. I'm over it. I liked hearing about you as a boy, though."

"What did you like about it?" He turned me over and then lied on top of me. My eyes were still closed, as I felt groggy. I wasn't sure of the answer and one wasn't required. He began to make love to me and I laughed lightly and smiled in pleasure and delight. We clung to each other like we were drowning. Neither of us was scared. And when it was over, neither of us let go. We were down there in the deep and it wasn't cold or turbulent. It was the most perfect way of existing. Sex had become life. He eventually pulled away with a groan and got ready for work. I stayed in bed, balled up in the sheet, and waited for his kiss good-bye. He came, sat on the bed, and stroked my cheek. My mouth opened like a baby expecting something to suck on. He watched me, with both love and lust, and I wasn't uncomfortable. Not at all.

He leaned down and kissed me on the mouth. "I love you." And then he left. I lingered, but then I groaned as William had, and after several minutes got out of bed, resentful that pedestrian life should interfere with the perfect sexual world I was in. Today, I was going to attempt to bleed my soul on the page. I had to be disciplined about it. I showered, dressed and was sitting in the office with my laptop by nine. I started by describing my apartment in Barcelona, where I was stationed in the military. As I dove in, I began remembering more and more, even the faces of my neighbors and the beer labels on the bottles they would pass to me when they invited me in for grilled meat and conversations in English. I didn't know writing was the key to remembering. If I had known, I would have been writing all along since my mind recoiled and forgot long years and days of my life. I began planning other things in my life to write about, mainly William, when the doorbell rang. I was startled as I had never heard anyone ring our doorbell other than our housekeeper, and she wasn't due for two more days. I had no idea who it could be. I went to the door and looked out. There was a man dressed in a flannel shirt and he had close cut hair with a smashed nose, as if it had been broken more than once. I didn't open the door.

"Can I help you?" I yelled.

"I'm one of your neighbors. I need to borrow one of your shovels. The handle on mine just broke."

His voice sounded genuine, friendly and he claimed he was a neighbor though I had never seen him. I hadn't really seen any of the neighbors so I couldn't be sure if he was or wasn't. I opened the door.

The man smiled. "The shovel is in the garage," I said.

"Okay." He stared at me expectantly.

"Come with me." I closed the door and thought William would be proud of me for helping out a neighbor. I went down the stairs and veered right for the two car garage. We never parked in it, as it was a sea of boxes consisting mostly of my belongings. I heard the gravel crunch behind me and when I got to the garage, I realized I forgot my keys. I turned and the man bashed me over the head with what I assumed were brass knuckles, as I saw a sliver of their curved shine. I collapsed, face forward, but was not unconscious. I flopped onto the gravel and a figure loomed. Matthew. Things were not going to go well. He squatted and grabbed one of my arms, which I seemed unable to move properly, and he jabbed me with a hypodermic needle. The Earth became blank.

Next, I was bouncing from bumps. I was in a tight, black cocoon and I was bouncing. There was just a thin noodle of light. As I focused on it, my consciousness began to recede and all was blank again. Next, I was being lifted out of something and carried. There was even more light as I was being carried and I saw, for only a moment, Vanessa's face. I tried to mouth "mom." I wanted to yell it, like I would've as an upset eight year old. I was laid down on something cushiony. I saw another syringe hover in the air and then a quick pinch in my arm. Blank.

Cobwebs were drifting away and the light of thought and perception took root. I tried to sit up. I was in an empty room. There was a mattress on the other side of the room. There were only two small windows high on the left wall. There was gray light and the whole room was gloomy and indistinct. There was pressure in my bladder. I had to pee. I collapsed onto the mattress and my head rolled right. I saw a toilet set in a recess and a clean, white sink. I struggled, with almost unbearable effort, to stand. I leaned on the wall and inched towards the toilet. When I reached it, the door opened and a man I had not seen before was standing in the doorway. He was looking at me with a dangerous grin. I froze. He waved his hand, as if to say "proceed". My bladder was seriously about to burst. I couldn't take a stand against the compromised privacy. I lifted my dress, pulled down my underwear and sat on the toilet. Despite having an audience, my bladder was not shy. It emptied and emptied. When I was done, I staggered off and collapsed back onto the mattress. My dress was still hiked up.

I awakened to hands on my breasts. The hands moved up and down and went further to my vagina. I pulled my eyes open and saw Matthew crouched down by me. His eyes looked dead.

"Are you a bitch like your sister?" he asked. "I didn't like her, at all."

I would have fought him if I could. Or at least rolled away from him. I was paralyzed and had to submit to his touching. After a few minutes, he wiped tears from my eyes and then opened a small, black case and pulled out a syringe. He injected me again and the blankness terrorized me.

I woke up thirsty and hungry. There was a bottle of water and a bag of chips next to the mattress. I fumbled with both and managed to both drink and eat. I had to pee again and struggled to the toilet. No one walked in this time. I went back and sat on the mattress, but my energy and strength waned and I collapsed. I wondered how long I had been there and if William was out looking for me. He would look for me. He wasn't going to sleep peacefully without me in our bed. I stopped thinking of him as I wanted to sob. William. The door opened and two young girls who were sobbing and weary, were dragged into the room by Matthew and the man who had knocked on my door. He was no longer in plaid, but sleek black. The girl he was dragging fought back but he punched her stomach repeatedly until she crumpled into a wet, sobbing ball on the concrete floor. The other girl looked like she was in shock. Matthew told her to sit but she didn't, so he punched her twice until she complied with the order. Her face was ashen and she looked like she was on the verge of retching. Matthew pulled the black case out of his back pocket and prepared a syringe. He injected both girls; neither put up a fuss. My thought was that it was unsanitary to use the same needle. Matthew seemed to read my thought as he came over to me, refilled the syringe, and injected me with the dirty needle. He patted my arm and blew a kiss.

I think I must have gotten a stiffer dose than the girls because when I woke up, still with a dead body, the girls were sitting on the mattress, shivering, talking softly and staring at me. The door slammed and Matthew was standing over me.

"It's your lucky day," he said. He unbuckled his belt. He put his knees on my mattress and then opened my legs, which I couldn't move. No, I yelled. It was just a hard breath. Not an indicator of struggle or disapproval. He didn't look me in the eye. He slapped me several times and I could see it was his attempt to get himself excited. It seemed to work as he positioned himself between my legs, unzipped his pants and then jammed himself into me. Despite the drugged state, I could still feel some physical pain. Matthew had used tremendous force because I was neither wet nor excited. It's one of the reasons rape is typically so brutal. It was a biological and mechanical issue with the body. As he thrust, I hoped he wouldn't come inside me. I had missed my birth control twice before being held captive in this malevolent place. It was, really, the only thing I was thinking. The drugs numbed nearly everything else, including panic and suffering. He was slamming into me and it was hurting me, except my brain really wasn't registering the pain. I started to think of William again. I stopped because the feeling of needing to sob overwhelmed me. Strange how nearly all thoughts and feelings were deadened. Not William though. He was like a hot knife to the soul. Matthew finished without a shutter or a flutter. It was hard business for him. I heard the girls crying. They were breathing frantically and wiping tears. I was a lesson for them. Rape would never be a distant idea for them. They could be next.

I was in a marred state, unclean and very near dead. A few thoughts bubbled. Humpty Dumpty. He was an egg and as Alice approached him, he looked more like a human. It was Alice that suggested the wall and the fall. A very human egg sat on a wall dividing two sides, and then the egg fell. Powerful forces tried to put him together. No luck. I guess you shouldn't send a horse for fine hand work. I had no idea why I was thinking of Humpty Dumpty until it occurred to me that he fell. Shattered and couldn't be fixed. I think, once and for all, I had plunged into an abyss. There was no coming back. Was it worth coming back? I thought of William and finally let myself sob.

Chapter 10

The sobbing went on and on. The man who came to my house threw open the door and then pulled me up. Another man was at the door and they both grabbed hold of me and took me down a long hall to a nicely furnished room draped in blues and maroons, and bedecked with brass and gold objects. The light was gray again and it could either be nearing night or daylight. The men situated me in a leather chair with high sides but a short back. My head flopped and I strained to keep it upright. The man who hit my head left, and the other man disappeared behind me. He likely took a seat against the wall or else he was preparing to bash me with a baseball bat. Why would anyone spill blood in this pretty room? As I righted my head, I could see Vanessa walking forward. Not towards me, but to a chair sitting several feet across from me.

"Hello, Petra. Are you well?" Her red hair, now colored by dye, was free flowing across her shoulders. From a distance she looked attractive as long as you couldn't see the hateful eyes and the network of wrinkles. That was one benefit to not having fair skin. You aged slower on the surface.

I was able to grimace. "I'm not." I wondered if she found the humor in the question.

"I wanted to talk to you for a few minutes. I have to leave shortly. I did want to have a word. I've been thinking about the Dobbs situation, and while I'm sorry it occurred, I'm more aware of why I was careless with you. One is never too old for clarity. When I was a child, I grew up in Pinetop-Lakeside to a mechanic father and a mother who worked as a grocery clerk. On the surface, they appeared to be an average American couple with standard tastes and interests. Father loved football, mother loved to knit, and they barbequed every chance they had during the spring and summer. They even had a large network of friends. Pinetop-Lakeside was even smaller back then and they prided themselves on knowing nearly everyone. There was a dark secret in my family. My father was being sexual with me. It was mostly fondling and touching until I was twelve and then there was sex. It continued until I graduated from high school and left. I didn't get far. I couldn't get far, I had no money. I met your father, John, at a donut shop. Can you believe that? I was sitting there eating five donuts and he came over, sat across from me, and offered me one of his donuts. There was a hole in my stomach then and it lasted until I gained twenty pounds. Your father never said much. He was a study in silence. He didn't say anything as I ate my donuts. He just drank his coffee and when I was done, asked me if I wanted more. I was staying in a rooming house and waitressing. I had no car. An impossible situation in this part of the world. John had a beautiful pick-up, and he started picking me up and taking me places. I needed him. It wasn't love. I paid him back by having sex with him and I cried because it was my first sexual experience outside of my father. I got pregnant with you not long after and John insisted we get married. He rented a tiny chalet in Greer and we began to live as man and wife. I wasn't happy. I was unfulfilled, and my true self had yet to emerge. And I was stuck with a child. The rest you know."

I blinked. "Touching story."

"It's why I was careless in placing you with Dobbs."

I straightened my neck that felt like it was melting. "You didn't place me. You traded me. Dobbs said so. For a name. You wanted out of Arizona and he gave you a name. I was payment. I've already explained this."

Vanessa stiffened. "I never did like your way of speaking." She looked at a tapestry on the wall. "I want to give you some kind of closure. Is there anything you want or need to know before..."

"Before?" My mouth was dry and the question sounded like a croak.

"You're going to die, Petra. No one knows about this place. I'm sure your husband is flexing his muscles and flashing his badge all over the White Mountains. He won't find you. Don't let it torment you. I ask again, is there anything you need to know?"

I already knew I was going to die. I wasn't sad for my life. I was sad for William. I truly hoped he'd find someone. I knew he would. I just wanted the woman to be special enough for him. My heart cleaved in two thinking about William, and I knew I couldn't do that to myself. I needed some freedom from suffering as I faced death.

"Tell me about my sister?" I asked.

Vanessa sighed. "She was considerably more poised and sophisticated than you. She had a very sheltered upbringing and was kept consummately safe. Her education was stellar, and even though she did not attend college she was, in my opinion, a scholar."

"Why did you murder her?"

"She betrayed God. God has the right to do whatever he wants with us. Her blood was mine to spill."

"How did she betray you?" I was getting some strength in my legs and I was able to extend my legs.

"She betrayed the business."

I thought about that. "Who are the girls in that room with me?"

Vanessa considered the question and then shrugged. "It doesn't matter anymore. I buy and sell girls. Those girls have been bought by me and will be sold. In an Internet bidding. It is ridiculously easy to sell a human beings on the Internet."

"That was the business you got into? Sex trafficking? Tyson Yeager set you up in sex trafficking?"

Her eyes flashed with anger. "Who told you that name? How do you know it?"

"Dobbs."

"What a fool. He used to buy girls from Yeager."

"I guess that's why they could never find any other victims. If they were sex trafficked, they were no one."

"Have you told anybody about Tyson Yeager?"

I wondered what the concern was. Was he still alive? I'd told William but I never heard anything from him so I don't think he looked him up. He probably didn't even remember the name.

"No," I said. I didn't want them going after William. "Is he important? Maybe I should've told someone."

Vanessa looked impatient. "Is there anything else?"

I was done asking her questions at the revival meeting. I was very simply trying to prolong my life.

"Why the religion?"

He face lit up in the brightening room. The gray outside the window had burnished with light. "The Bible is poetic. The words simply burn on the page, and if you have any question, however small, you can find it in the scripture. I do find that many religions are squeamish about sex and do not fully appreciate femaleness on display."

"Women are on display all the time in our society."

"Women are on display purely as sex objects. They are not on display as sacred, holy or worthy of worship. Not when their sex is on display." She had the impassioned zeal of a professor.

"Was Kristin worthy of worship while she was on that cross?"

"Anyone on a cross is." Her patience was waning.

"But was Kristin?" I pressed.

"I absolved her of her sins when she died on that cross."

"That was kind of you."

"I'm done. Matthew?" She called out.

"What fixed the hole in your stomach?" I tried to flex my arms and grimaced when they flopped.

"Excuse me?"

"All the donuts?"

"Rage. I had a conversation with my father and threatened to turn him in. Oh, your grandparents are still alive and in Pinetop. Carl and Trish Connors. I guess it doesn't matter since you're dying shortly."

She stood up as Matthew approached. She hugged him and nestled her face on his chest. He ran his hands through her hair and kissed her forehead. It was too cute, as long as you forgot Matthew was a rapist maniac and Vanessa was a deranged damaged woman focused on killing her children. Otherwise, they were perfect for each other. He led Vanessa to the room's entry and she stretched her neck back and peered at me. I thought she looked sad.

"Good-bye Petra."

"One last question," I said. Vanessa looked annoyed.

"Why Petra? The real reason. Not your made up reason of me shaking and looking petrified."

"It means stone or rock. I gave it to you in hopes it would give you strength and help you survive the brutal world." She was walked out of the room with her arm still encircling Matthew. I didn't always thrive in the brutal world, but I did survive it.

My head was less wobbly and I thought I could stand. I pushed off with my hands. I lifted myself up a few inches and then slammed back down onto the chair. From behind, I felt arms grip me tightly, and I was lifted off the chair to a standing position. The fingers of the men holding me tightly burrowed deep into my flesh painfully and uncomfortably. Matthew reappeared and gone was the dreamy look of his love for Vanessa.

"Take her out back."

Matthew turned and the men moved me forward. I let my legs go slack, making them even more useless. It didn't seem to impact them. They had large muscles and the movement forward did not cease. I was starting to feel panic, a primitive panic. The panic one experiences in facing annihilation. I was taken out into the sun. The air was soft, almost velveteen. The slight chill in the air was steadily being burned off by the insistent spring rays. I was taken across the immense yard to a place near the woods. I could smell the delicious pine scent. On the ground was a monstrous cross. I was to be crucified, and panic gave way to crystalline fear whose crystals were more aggravatingly intoxicating than the drugs. Except fear did not blanket me in blankness. It sizzled my mind and body and forced me to start weeping. How horrible to be sacrificed. Was Jesus consoled by the fact he was dying for something? Nonsense. There is no abstract thought on the gallows. The men began taking my clothes off and I fought by keeping my limbs as rigid as I could.

"Your death is about choices." Matthew had moved from the head of the cross.

"Your first choice. Do you want more drugs or do you wish to suffer on the cross? You will have consciousness and be able to take in the last bits of the world."

I thought about that. I had no appetite for suffering. I didn't want to long for the world for however long it took for me to die.

"Drugs…" I said haltingly.

"I thought you might."

He went over to a picnic table sitting a few yards away. On it was his trusted compact zippered case and from its Velcro snaps he withdrew another syringe that he filled with a small vial, also secured by Velcro enclosures. As he injected me, I noted his eyes were still dead looking and had fully lost the gloss that shone from them when he was with Vanessa. My training in the police and interrogation was pushing me to engage him in conversation in order to delay what was inevitable. However, the drugs and futility kept me quiet, and though it may seem like I was accepting death, I most definitely was not. All the fibers and sinews in me were screeching, even as they gave over to the drug.

The men laid my nude body over the cross. I was feeling less and less self-conscious about my nakedness. The quirkiness of the drug. I gazed into the yellowy gold sky and attempted to consume the Earth one last time. I noted the chirping of birds and then rustling somewhere in the woods. It was likely a squirrel or chipmunk.

"Your next choice. Do you want the nails in your wrist or hands?"

Who can answer such a question? If you hang by your hands then your hands cannot support your weight. A nail in a wrist is a better choice but I couldn't stomach, even with the drug, the thought of a nail through my wrist.

"Hand..."

The word was barely formed. The drug was seizing up body functions and slowly blanketing the brain with cotton.

"Suit yourself."

One of the men handed Matthew a long, fat, piercing nail. I looked into the sky, and felt my tears cooled on my face by a velvet breeze and then felt a wrenching, scorching, unbelievable pain in my hand that caused me to wail. I felt vomit gurgle in my throat and I attempted to spit it out.   Vomit and bile ebbed and flowed down my neck and chest.

"Ready for another one?" Matthew asked.

I was done communicating. I wanted to be alone in my pain. Matthew extended my other arm on the cross. He worked on positioning it right in the middle of the wood. I closed my eyes and then I heard yelling. Strange voices. From far away. Somebody yelled Sheriff's Department. I figured I was hallucinating. And then men communicated with Matthew and they became feverish and then I heard horrible booms. Gunfire. I opened my eyes and saw the two men lying on the grass several feet away.

"Fuck you, Petra."

Matthew searched in his pockets. He was looking for a nail. I assumed. Or maybe it was his case with the syringe? I realized he didn't have a weapon on him. In frustration he raised the hammer with the intention of slamming it down on my skull, but his head exploded, raining blood and brain matter down on me. Through the red wetness covering my eyes I saw William. That's when I heard Vanessa screaming. I

thought I could hear her footfalls across the grass, but William turned and shot her in

the mid-section. I did see she was wielding something. If William shot her, it was likely a

gun. I felt an overflowing happiness that William shot my mother. It seemed like a

Greek tragedy. There was then a flood of deputies and other law enforcement

converging on the house and the yard. William bent down and wiped blood from my

face.

"Can you hang in there? We need to wait for the paramedics. They're coming by

helicopter. We have to figure out what to do with this nail. I'll find something to clean

you with." His voice was concerned and so soothingly calm that I want to kiss him,

except the nail in my hand prevented movement and a blood and bile-covered face was

abhorrent.

I said, "Druuug…"

William looked confused and then, apparently noting my virtually paralyzed

limbs, understood. I was under the influence of some drug.

He stroked my head. "You'll be alright. I love you. You'll be alright."

In his presence, I felt safety, warmth and the relief of being spared death. I felt

my mind caving inwards and giving up its stranglehold on reality. As I slipped into

unconsciousness, I thought of the ending of *The Threepenny Opera*. Macheath was

sentenced to die and as he stood on the gallows, he received a pardon by the queen and

the hanging apparatus was deemed faulty and inoperable. Macheath was spared and

walked on into a suddenly cheering crowd. He was rescued. Mrs. Peachum noted that

people usually aren't saved. The magical way out almost never happens. And yet I was saved from death on a cross, under the protection of William and soon to be airborne on the way to the hospital. It was magic. Or maybe it was love. Was there a difference?

Chapter 11

I selected the Shutters in Santa Monica. It was expensive. William didn't make a comment. Of course, he had investment money from the fund his brother managed. But I wasn't going to make him pay. My house had finally sold and I was flush with cash. I had money to blow. I chose Shutters because it was on the beach, had a beautiful pool, and beachy-looking rooms. I also chose LA County for our California trip and not Orange County. I wanted to be far from his family and friends.

It was less than two months since our last California trip. I couldn't stay in the White Mountains. I felt like ripping my hair out. Our home was no longer a safe Eden we retreated too. Someone had assaulted the sacredness of its confines. I had also become infamous in our area. I was a victim of a crime twice in the span of a few months. My picture ran in local and national press. I was touted as a victim in a sex trafficking ring. It was both true and inaccurate. People assumed I was being sex trafficked. I was recognized all over the White Mountains, and it wasn't always with effusive sympathy. Marge responded to me with chilly compassion and I hoped beyond hope that I wouldn't have to suffer through another awkward dinner. I had to leave with or without William. William understood and asked the retired Sheriff Morris to take over for two weeks. Morris was actually quite friendly to me and didn't seem to mind that he was having to set aside retirement so William could take off to California. He seemed to understand that I had to escape.

I spent several days in the hospital. It wasn't due to my injured hand, which required minor surgery and physical therapy. It was the drugs. Heavy dosing of heroin. When the last dose Matthew gave me wore off I went through withdrawals, which was closely monitored.

I wasn't bothered by the Sheriff's Department while I was undergoing the withdrawals. My brain was still considered altered. Immediately after I was cleared, Marge and Clive showed up with their notebooks and I provided my statement and relayed everything I could remember. One thing stuck in my throat, though.

"Is there anything else?" Marge asked.

"There is," I said.

I considered the best way of saying what I needed to say. Clive's piggy face looked earnest and eager to listen. Marge's moon face looked reticent and beleaguered, and yet she still seemed professional with a vague whiff of being supportive.

"Matthew…he…Matthew raped me. There's no easy way of saying it."

I then explained the incident in detail. Both deputies looked concerned and sympathetic.

"Can you do me a favor? Can you let me tell William before he hears it from you two or reads it in a report?"

Marge and Clive said they could do that and then left my room. William was working. He was trying to wrap up all the issues with the case. More leads had to be investigated to ferret out the sex traffickers and track down any of the girls. He spent nights with me on a cot. Phone calls would still come in and it was difficult for him as he was not allowed to use his cell phone on the floor.

He came in with two thick folders that night and a stern expression that melted when he kissed me. I gently recoiled when he kissed me. I didn't know why and William noticed, but he was far too tenderhearted to say anything. He threw the folders on the cot and sat in the bedside chair and stared at the TV that was off. You could see our shadows on the screen.

"I wanted to ask you..."

"Hmmm."

"How did you know where to find me?"

William leaned forward and braced his elbows near his knees and cupped his face in his hands. "Tyson Yeager. You told me about him. I didn't look into it at the time. After a day of searching for you, I concentrated on the things you told me. When I looked into him it was not an alarming history. He lived here up until five years ago when he died. He was originally from Louisiana. That interested me as the wood from Kristin's cross came from there. There really aren't coincidences. He owned a series of bars in the White Mountains and the ones he owned were known for women. Prostitutes. He was never seriously investigated. He was occasionally watched. The fact your mother became involved with him made things interesting. I discovered there was still a property, far out from Eagar and Springerville, which was still under his name. I asked the District Attorney for a statement of his Probate and it was disclosed your mother was the Executor. I wasn't sure what I was walking into so I gathered all the manpower I could and we converged."

"How did it feel shooting Medusa?"

William turned and put a hand over mine. "I'm sorry I had to do that. She was running at me with a gun. How do you feel about it?"

"Glad." She died in the air on the way to the hospital. "But how did it make you feel?"

"A part of me was pleased. She did a great deal of harm to you."

I patted his hand. "Believe me. I'm happy."

We grew quiet and I knew I had to fill the void with unpleasantness.

"I gave my statement to Marge and Clive."

"Good. Hopefully, that closes out your part. I have to face a hearing on the shooting but they aren't going to call you as you're my wife."

"Okay. I did tell Marge and Clive something that will end up in the report and increase the number of crimes. It involves me."

"A crime you committed?"

"No. Please listen. I'm not sure how to tell and you aren't going to be happy. I just hope you aren't mad at me, for some reason. When I was still very drugged, Matthew came in and…he…well, he…fuck…he raped me. Those two girls were witnesses. I couldn't fight back as my body wasn't cooperating and I wasn't even registering any real pain. I…I…wanted to tell you instead of you reading it in a report."

William was quiet as he gazed at my heavily bandaged hand.

"Thank you for telling me." His voice was compassionate. "I already knew. We interviewed the two girls a few days ago."

"You knew and didn't say anything?" I wasn't angry. I was confused.

"Would you have wanted me to say something? Whether you tell me or not is up to you. I'm surprised you made an argument for yourself not fighting back. That's concerning, Petra. Even if you weren't drugged, you didn't have to fight back. You're blaming yourself. It's going to make it difficult for you to recover."

"What did the girls say?"

William stood and fussed with my blanket. "What does it matter?"

"What did they say, William?"

He stopped tugging at the blanket and looked at me frankly. "They said it was brutal and it was greatly disturbing to both of them."

Tears, not called upon, flooded my eyes and splashed all over my face. William looked traumatized and tormented. I knew he wanted to hold me, but he knew I no longer wanted to be touched or rather, enveloped, by his arms. Abusers take everything. William turned off the overhead light and turned on a small lamp that provided enough light for him to read his files but not enough light to disturb my slumber..

I was released four days later. William worked from home. I was thankful because I did not want to be in the house by myself. I was either in bed or in the den watching TV. Our refrigerator was stocked with food that William had instructed the housekeeper to buy. She outperformed, and was likely happy to not be cleaning and instead focusing her attention on shopping. There was no reason to leave the house.

The housekeeper had set the Bertolt Brecht picture in William's office. He was sitting at his desk typing on the computer when I walked in.

"What is your intention for that picture?" he asked.

"Intention? I just like having it. Maybe it can go in the den."

"Brecht does not match my Americana hunting décor."

"You don't even hunt. It's a false décor."

"That leaves Americana."

"Brecht was in America. Los Angeles." I explained the history. William's eyes glazed. I figured I'd told the story before.

"We should go to LA. Soon."

William nodded. He was considering it. "I think it should go in the den."

The picture stayed sitting in his office. It reminded me that I was still in his home, the home he bought and decorated. I made a note to call my broker and suspend the sale.

The next morning I called my broker and she was excited.

"We have a buyer. They have an offer."

The offer was my $4,000 below my asking price.

"It's a start." I said I would consider it. I went into the bedroom where William was folding clothes. My hand injury prevented any such task. I told him I had an offer on the house.

"That's wonderful." He laid a t-shirt onto a towering stack of folded ones. I frowned.

"It's not wonderful?" he asked.

"Is this really my home?" I asked.

He looked calm. "Why would you ask that?"

"All my stuff is sitting in the garage. You won't even let me hang a single picture?"

"This is about Brecht? You can hang Brecht wherever you want." He started folding a pair of pants.

"It's the idea of Brecht."

"The idea?" The pants became a neat square.

"He took other people's work and made it his own. He put his own creativity into it. They became masterpieces."

"You want to put your creativity into this house? Do it."

He said it too quickly.

"You don't mean it."

William took his hand and swatted the stack of t-shirts, which caused them to fall into a messy pile on the floor. I was alarmed, as I had never seen him do anything like that.

"Why would you even ask if this your home? Fuck, Petra. We're married. Did you forget that?"

"No, I just feel like you're trying to contain me in a neat box."

"When you spill out and get messy, look what happens." I could see his chest rising and falling.

"You're blaming me for everything that's happened?" I was incredulous.

"In chasing down the past, you put yourself in danger."

"The past is over. I know what I need to know. And you aren't upset about that. It's the rape. You're upset about that."

His eyes widened in surprise. "What're you talking about?"

I didn't know. It was on my mind. How did things go from being perfect with William to fucked? Captivity and rape.

"Forget it." I turned to leave but he caught hold of my hand and was careful not to pull me close to him. Sometimes he forgot that I had alarming memories of Matthew.

"We should leave. I have to make arrangements and this case has to settle down. Maybe two weeks."

I nodded.

"I'm most definitely not upset with you about the rape. I'm extremely angry with your mother and the asshole who did it. No one's blaming you, Petra. You're blaming yourself."

I knew I was.

I accepted the offer on the house and the buyer paid cash. We left three weeks later and the house proceedings were in my account on our drive to California. For our first few days there, I begged William to take me to every major museum including the Norton-Simon in Pasadena. It was at the Getty, a museum jutting far above the 405 freeway and overlooking the Pacific, that I felt a sensation akin to peace. It wasn't overwhelming, but it was significant. I nestled into William's surprised arms. We didn't say anything as we gazed at the sprawling coastline. We got back to the hotel and I insisted on a walk on the beach. The sun was setting and it would be the ideal time. I was less focused on the look of the ocean than I was on remembering the smell. There was also the feel of William's hand on my shoulder. I wanted to remember that.

Five days into our stay, I had a problem that was confirmed by a trip to the drug store and a restroom while William slept in. I got back to the hotel room feeling crushed. William woke up, as if sensing my presence.

"Hey, I want to go to Orange County. I want to introduce you to my parents." I started sobbing. "What's wrong?"

"I...I...I'm pregnant."

William scrutinized me for several seconds. "Am I supposed to be upset? I'm not. I'm actually thrilled."

"You don't understand. I think its Matthew's." I whispered the name.

"But it could be mine..."

"Yes, but..."

William closed his eyes and laid his head down on his pillow. "Do you want an abortion? I can take you to a clinic. I can take you today. I think there's pills now. When it's early on. Not sure."

My crying subsided. "You would do that?"

He closed his eyes. "Whatever you want, Petra." There was a hardness to his body. He was like a corpse under the sheet.

I washed my face and brushed my hair. I was ready to go. William was still in bed, facing the blonde wood shutters that opened onto our balcony. I turned off the light in the bathroom.

"I'm ready." I walked along the edge of the bed. I was afraid to look at him. I sighed and climbed into my side of the bed.

"William." I touched his blanketed shoulder. "I don't want his child."

He rolled over to lie flat. "They can do tests. Later." He furrowed his brow in concentration. "Do you want the child if it's mine?"

That was the more significant issue. I was still ambivalent to children. However, William looked crestfallen at the prospect of an abortion of his child. He wasn't ambivalent. Not at all. And the prospect of his aborted DNA made him look miserable. Maybe that's what happens in a relationship; you sacrifice for the one you love. I knew not having his child would destroy a part of our relationship and I had to consider that I had been casual with the birth control pills in the few days prior to being taken into captivity. Why was that? In the past, I had been zealous about birth control. The fault is in our fibers. That's why things happen. Internal forces not external ones. I had made a choice. A repeated choice.

I curled into his body and he wasn't unyielding.

"Let me think about it." I rubbed my hand across his stomach and he grabbed hold of it and kissed it. "If we had a child, we would need a bigger house. And Brecht is going up."

"You can put Brecht in any room of the house."

"Then it's going in your office." I thought for a moment. "Don't tell anybody, anything until we know about the DNA."

"You have to be far along to do the test."

"Oh." I knew nothing about pregnancy.

"You can say you miscarried. Not aborted."

"Oh."

"We can look for a new house?" William's face was beaming.

He looked happy and I knew I couldn't crush that. "We can look for a new house, as long as the decorating is a joint project."

"Americana," he said with a grin.

"Weimar." I had no idea what that would look like.

"Americana Weimar. Done."

And then I kissed my still very new husband.

A few days later, I asked where my sister was buried and William said Show Low. Vanessa never claimed her body. A week later I drove to the cemetery with William. I had the Brecht photo with me. I left the frame in the garage. William didn't know I had it. I laid pale pink roses on her flat grave marker and unfurled Brecht and placed him underneath the roses.

"Is that…"

"Yes. I think we both liked Brecht."

"Oh."

"Do you know what I'm going to do?"

"Belt out Mack the Knife?" He looked earnest.

"Write. That's what I'm going to do. And I'm going to start with the night we met."

"Make sure you share everything." His face looked amused.

"I will, I will." I took his hand into mine and noted that peace had dropped into my soul.

About the Author

R.C. Peris was born and raised in Southern California, the home of brush fires and blanket-like smog. She currently lives in Arizona with her existential minded chickens. This is her second full-length novel. She is also a screenwriter, playwright, poet, and artist.

To learn more: www.rcperis.com

Facebook: https://www.facebook.com/periswriter

Facebook Art Page: Art of R.C. Peris

Twitter: @periswriter

www.ingramcontent.com/pod-product-compliance
Lightning Source LLC
Chambersburg PA
CBHW070946190726
48292CB00004B/1353